Fairy Tales
FROM THE GARDEN

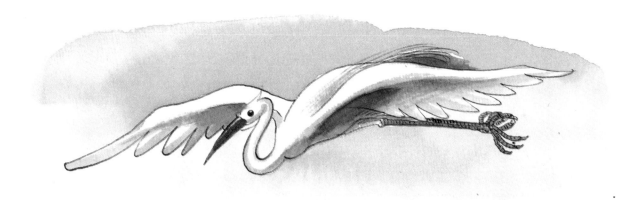

Fairy Tales

From
The
Garden

Text by Vratislav Šťovíček

Illustrations by Zdenka Krejčová

Designed and produced by Aventinum

This edition published 1993 by Sunburst Books, Deacon House,
65 Old Church Street, London, SW3 5BS, and exclusively for
Coles in Canada

Text by Vratislav Šťovíček
Translated by Louise Doležalová
Illustrated by Zdenka Krejčová
Graphic design by Alena Beldová
© Aventinum, Prague 1992

ISBN   1 85778 027 2

Printed in the Slovak Republic by Neografia, Martin
1/20/12/51-01

Contents

The Queen of the Flowers

A very long time ago, the kingdom of the flowers was ruled by the sleepy King Lotus. Deep in his dreams, he rocked endlessly on the waves of the lake and did not care at all for his subjects. Very soon the flowers lost patience and appealed to the heavens to send them a new ruler, but their voices were so soft they could not be heard high above. So they asked the nightingale to rise high above the clouds and carry their wishes to the heavens. The nightingale was glad to help. As soon as he had delivered the message, a small bud came down from above, floated to the ground, there unfolding into a pure white rose, surrounded by thorns. The rose was so beautiful that the bird messenger fell in love with it at first sight. He sped from the clouds to be closer to the rose and snuggled against it, but as he did so, the merciless thorns sank deep into his breast and the nightingale's blood fell on the rose's petals and coloured the flower crimson. From that time, roses of different colours have grown on

earth, but only the one whose colour is the same as the nightingale's blood is the true queen of the flowers.

Early one winter, as the last flower fairies and gnomes left their sleeping gardens to take refuge in the winter garden of the Rose Queen, their ruler decided to hold a wonderful gala flower ball in her royal palace. It was to last until the magic pipe of the merry god Pan could be heard signalling merrily that far away, in the land of people, Spring was on its way.

Thousands of wondrous flowers from all over the world gathered there. In this magical place, the flowers took on different forms. The longer they were there, the more they began to look like fairies or graceful princesses in sumptuous gowns with trains set with dewdrop gems. Some of them became fairytale princes in brightly coloured jackets and tunics made from petals, or like proud knights in shining armour and plumes of blossom above their haughty brows. In the shade of the royal garden stately court

the towers of the royal palace could be seen to shine brightly in the lights of thousands of fireflies. Amid a fanfare, the Rose Queen herself came to take her place on a golden throne. She signalled for the music to start and all the flowers in the ballroom and garden began to dance. If you could have seen it from above, it looked like a breeze rippling through an almost endless, brightly coloured flowerbed. In the heat of the dance the flowers turned their faces to the sprays of the rainbow fountains and allowed their heated brows to be fanned by the delicate wings of butterflies which settled in their hair.

As the dance ended, the Rose Queen clapped her tiny hands and her high, clear voice rang out into the silence, 'I welcome you, my dear guests. I hope you will enjoy many beautiful days and nights at our gala flower ball, but I have one small request. I would like to ask each of you, during this time, to grant me a request. I have a wish for fairytales, so before the end of the ball you must come to me with a story from a far off corner of the world. At the end of our ball

ladies in frothy crinolines walked. Eastern beauties in kimonos of cobweb shyly hid their smiles behind birdfeather fans, while restless little princesses held up their skirts and walked barefoot through the dewy grass, making fun of the water lily fairies as they passed by the little lakes where they grew. Inside meadows, pageboys amused themselves by figuring with little swords made of sharply pointed thorns and little archers shot arrows of dandelion down high into the sky.

At the end of the day, as the sun went down,

we will decide which of them was the most beautiful. Who will be the first?'

The flowers looked at each other in bewilderment. No one had the courage to start. A tiny princess with a violet crown in her hair hurried so fast to hide herself away in a corner that she lost her satin slipper on the way. In embarrassment she crept back. The Rose Queen saw her, and spoke to her, smiling.

'Princess Violet, favourite flower of Empress Josephine, what are you afraid of? Little flower of romance, you who are the herald of spring, have you nothing to say to us? I have heard that you were born from Adam's tears. I have also heard that you are the secret messenger of love, so please don't be shy,' the Queen entreated her.

Princess Violet was so timid and shy that did not know which way to look, but when the Rose Queen kindly hugged her, she plucked up her courage and quietly, in a tiny voice, began her story.

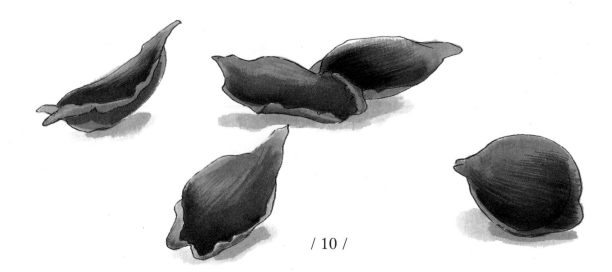

The Gardener Prince

There was once a king who had three sons. The two elder ones were so strong and brave that no one, near or far, could match them. As for the youngest one, it was whispered around the castle that the good fairies were probably sleeping when he was born. He was not very strong and he was also quite timid. He did not speak much, preferring to stroll around the royal garden, enjoying the sights, sounds and smells, and caring for the plants, trees and flowers. He watered the flowers every day, and listened to the birdsong for hours on end. Soon he became known all over the Kingdom as the Gardener Prince.

One day, the king called his sons to him and spoke. 'I am old and tired,' he said. 'It seems that I shall soon be leaving to join your mother in Heaven. I should therefore be glad if you would each find for yourself a bride. High up in the Black Tower is a chamber in which you will find statues of the loveliest girls anyone has ever seen. Choose the one that you like most. The one to make the best choice will take my place as king and the ruler of this land.'

The sons obediently took from their father a golden key, unlocked the gate to the Black Tower and climbed the long spiral staircase.

After an almost endless climb, they found themselves in a splendid room. Instead of a ceiling the starlit sky rose over their heads, and beneath their feet flowers of every colour bloomed in velvet grass. Wherever they looked there were statues of young girls so beautiful that the princes gasped in wonder. The statues were cast in pure gold and silver and royal crowns of pearls and diamonds sparkled on their lovely brows. The bewitched young men wandered helplessly from statue to statue but just couldn't make up their minds. They couldn't decide which of the girls was the most beautiful of all.

Then the Gardener Prince found a statue standing all alone in a far off corner. Covering the figure was a long black cloth. When the young prince pulled the cloth away, he and his

brothers were struck dumb with surprise. Before them stood the most beautiful statue they had ever seen. This statue was different from all the rest in that it was made entirely from ice. A bright crown of snow flakes shone above her downcast face and real tears flowed from her gentle eyes.

The eldest brother was the first to come to his senses. 'That's the one I want for my wife and no other,' he cried. 'It will go badly for anyone who stands in my way,' he warned.

The middle brother grasped his sword in anger. 'You have no greater right to her than I. If you won't give way, then I shall have to fight you for her.'

If it hadn't been for the Gardener Prince, the angry brothers would have set upon each other.

'My brothers,' he said smiling, 'let us not quarrel. Only she has the right to decide. Let us go, in turn, out into the world to look for this lovely girl. She will belong for ever only to the one who wins her heart.' Turning to the eldest prince he said, 'You, brother, were the first of us to see her in the light of day, so you must be the first to search for her in the world.'

The eldest brother was ashamed of his quick temper and thanked the young prince for his kindness. However, when he told the king of his intentions, the old man frowned. 'You have not made a wise decision, my sons. Beyond seven mountains and seven rivers stands the ice palace. There you will find the girl of your choice, the princess from the country of Eternal Spring. The ruler of the snow realm changed her into an icy statue because she refused to become his wife. Only the man who can lay the most precious gifts in the world at her feet will succeed in breaking the spell and transform her into a living woman once again. Anyone who fails will himself be turned into a statue of ice. Many courageous princes have tried their luck but no one has yet returned.'

The eldest son was not deterred by his father's words. Without delay, he summoned to the castle the best jewellers and goldsmiths in the land and ordered them to fashion for him a rose of pure gold. When the craftsmen had completed their work, all those who saw it gazed in wonder. The petals of the flower were so delicate that they were stirred by a baby's sigh. Inside the flower an emerald butterfly

sighed. 'But if you put it on your head, in a trice you will find yourself just where you want to be. Before you leave, however, thrust your sword into the ground. You will not need it on your journey. If your sword becomes rusty we shall know that you have met with misfortune.' The young man did as his father directed, and the moment he donned the cap, disappeared as if the earth had closed over him.

Not much time had passed when, one morning, the old king found that his son's sword was covered in rust. In vain he tried to persuade his middle son to give up his search. Instead, straight away the young man called for the most famous artists in the land. He ordered them to create a portrait of himself in precious stones. When the artists had finished their work, no one could believe their eyes. The prince's face seemed to come alive. The diamond hair blew in the breeze, alabaster lids were half-closed over eyes of pearl and a cunning smile curved the ruby lips. The old king was content.

'Your gift is even more beautiful than your elder brother's. Perhaps God will grant you luck.' The prince then chose the silver chest on the advice of the king and found in it a jester's slippers with little bells on them.

'When you put those slippers on, your feet will be keener than your senses. In the winking of an eye they will carry you to where you want to be,' said the king, 'but it would be wiser not to hurry.' The middle son took no heed of his warning. Just as the eldest brother had done, he too, thrust his sword into the ground in front of the gate, pulled on the slippers and disappeared. One day the king noticed that the second son's sword had also become rusty. In sorrow, he gave the sad news to the Gardener Prince. He would not let himself be dissuaded from the journey, either.

fluttered its feather-light wings and around the rose a silver nightingale hovered. The old king was pleased with the gift for the girl.

'Perhaps you will be successful, my son. This rose is beautiful. Any woman would be delighted to receive it,' he said and then led the prince to three chests. The first was made of gold, the second was made of silver and the third was made of ordinary oak wood.

'Open the one of your choice,' the king commanded. With no hesitation the prince raised the lid of the gold chest and looked with surprise at the cap and bells of a jester.

'That cap will not give you wisdom,' his father

'Have you chosen the most precious gift in the world for your bride?' the king asked. The prince shook his head.

'Perhaps something will occur to me on the way,' he answered carelessly. When he opened the oak chest, he found only a withered bunch of violets at the bottom.

'I have nothing to give you for the journey,' the king sighed. 'What you are looking at are the first violets which I picked with love a long time ago for your mother. I have kept them all this time.'

The prince's heart leapt with joy.

'Thank you, father. You have no idea how you have helped me. Now I know what is the most precious gift in the world.' With these words, he hurriedly said goodbye to the old king and set out into the world. He walked over seven mountains and waded through seven rivers, but was still not at the end of his journey.

One day he arrived at a marvellous magic tree. Golden blossoms shone from its branches and above it hovered diamond bees. On the topmost branch sat a strange bird whose feathers sparkled like the sun. Around its neck was a rainbow coloured ribbon.

'Welcome, Prince,' said the bird in a human voice. 'I know where you are going. I am the Guardian of the Tree of Wealth. My tree will fulfil the most secret wish of all those who reach it. Do you know already the most precious gift in the world?'

The Gardener Prince smiled.

'Riches mean nothing to me,' he said. 'Beneath your tree of gold the humble violet blooms. Will you allow me to pick a bunch of them for my bride, the ice maiden, for the most precious of all gifts is a gift given with love.'

'You have chosen wisely, young man,' said the bird, and when the Prince had made ready

a little bunch of violets for his bride, the bird called to him to catch hold of its rainbow ribbon. Together they flew up into the air, and before long they saw the ice palace far lying beneath them.

Down, down, down, they flew and landed with a small bump in the courtyard of the palace. The Prince saw before him a long icy stairway. The Gardener Prince thanked the bird who wished him good luck, and was gone. Slowly and carefully he began his journey up the stairway and into the palace, pausing to steady himself once or twice on the way. There sat the ice maiden on a throne of snowflakes with dozens of glorious gifts at her feet, and surrounded by suitors of all kinds who were now just pillars of ice. Among their number were the brothers of the Gardener Prince.

The Prince knelt solemnly before the throne and placed the little bunch of violets in the princess's hands.

'Please accept my simple gift, dear princess. It is a gift given with true love.'

At that moment, the princess's heart began to beat once more, her cheeks grew rosy and she smiled as though waking from a dream. Then, all the other icy statues began to wake, and where only a few moments before there had been nothing but cold silence, a new warmth spread through the company.

'You were the only one to realize what is the most precious gift in the world,' the princess said. 'I know you must truly love me and I know I love you. If you want, I'll become your wife.'

So the Gardener Prince and his beautiful bride set out for home at the head of a distinguished procession of many princes and noblemen. The old king welcomed his lost sons with open arms and arranged for his youngest son a wedding which everyone remembers to this day. For thirty days and nights they toasted the health and happiness of the Gardener Prince and his lovely wife and when, at last, the final piece of wedding cake had been eaten in the kitchen by the kitchen boy, the Gardener Prince returned unseen to the oak chest and in it, right at the bottom, placed a withered bunch of violets.

Princess Camomile

The Rose Queen clapped her hands, the music stopped playing and, bowing charmingly, the dancers led their partners to cushions of soft moss. It was time for a fairytale. The Rose Queen looked around and then beckoned with her fan to a little golden-haired girl wearing a shining white crown. 'I will tell you a story,' she said shyly. 'Listen.'

Once upon a time, in the middle of a green meadow, lay a flourishing kingdom where a golden king and a silver queen had ruled as long as the world had existed. People were born and died, the years rolled on and away, but the royal couple never grew old. They remained as young and beautiful as ever, for they were immortal.

One day the king found his wife leaning on a cushion on the window and crying her heart out. 'I want to die,' she sobbed, 'we have been ruling our kingdom from age to age, we can recall much happiness and much sorrow and our hearts grow heavier all the time. Those we have loved died long ago. Only we two are condemned to live till the end of the world.' The king tried in vain to console her.

'Why can't we be like other people whose lives have a beginning and an end?' she sighed.

Sadly, the king took from a chest the Book of

Life. It was written on thousands of flower petals from all over the world. It shone with a thousand colours and was fragrant with thousands of perfumes.

'Listen to what is written here,' said the king and read in a quiet voice, 'I, the Book of Life, reveal my secret to the golden king and the silver queen. They will become mortal only when their daughter marries a young prince, the new ruler of the kingdom.'

When the queen heard this, she cried even more. 'We have been waiting from age to age, my lord, for a child to smile at us from her cradle, but it seems that we are not destined to have such luck. Our cradle is empty.'

At last the queen, worn out from sorrow, was overcome by sleep. In her sleep she heard a whisper. 'The poor silver queen,' said the voice. 'She does not know that she could have a daughter within a year if only she would drink the dew from our flowers at dawn. This is not written in the Book of Life.'

Sleepily, the queen opened her eyes and looked out of the window into the garden, but she saw only the delicate white bloom of the Lily and nearby the modest Wormwood flower.

'I had a dream,' she thought and once again her eyelids closed. This time she fell into such a deep sleep that the Wormwood flower's answer did not reach her ears. 'You are right, sister Lily,' whispered the Wormwood flower, 'but in time, the queen's happiness would turn into endless sorrow. Is it not true that what comes from the earth returns to the earth? When her time came, the young princess, to the grief of her parents, would change into a flower again. Be glad that the Book of Life remains silent about our secret.'

'You speak wisely, brother,' the Lily nodded and the flowers fell silent.

The silver queen slept for a long time. It was dawn when she woke. Silently, she returned into the crisp morning air. Remembering her dream, she knelt by the flowers and saw that they were full of sparkling dew. 'It was only a dream,' she sighed wistfully, but she could not help herself and drank the dew from the chalices of the Lily and Wormwood. Lo and behold, in that moment her sadness disappeared like the morning mist and the queen's face glowed with joy as never before. Less than a year passed before a little girl, pretty as a picture, smiled back at her from the royal cradle. She had golden hair and a snow-white crown rested on her radiant brow. She reminded the king and queen so much of a flower that they called her Camomile.

Time passed and the little girl grew into a lovely young woman. So beautiful was she that soon princes and knights began to travel to the royal castle from all parts of the world to win her favours in valiant tournaments. However, Princess Camomile became more and more reserved, preferring to wander alone through the meadows where she played with the butterflies that settled in her hair. A rumour soon spread through the kingdom that the royal daughter was really a beautiful witch. It was said that she could talk to the flowers. In vain, the well-born suitors tried to flatter their way into her favour, but to no avail.

'Don't expect me to fall for any one of you. I am Camomile, daughter of the flowers. I smell as sweetly as love and bitter, very bitter as sorrow. I should not bring you good fortune,' she said to the princes who came to court her. She spoke with such sadness in her voice that they had no choice but to believe her, and silently they all set off for home.

The story of the sad princess soon spread throughout the world and no one found the courage any more to try for her hand. The roads to the castle remained deserted, and the golden king and the silver queen were desolate. Then one day, a young, golden-haired prince in diamond encrusted armour came into the courtyard. He bowed to the royal parents and knelt before the Princess Camomile. 'I saw your face in the mirror of the moon,' he said. 'You are as lovely as a flower of the meadow. Please be my wife.'

Camomile held her breath and could not take her eyes off the prince, but then tears appeared on her cheeks. 'I do like you and I should be happy to promise to marry you. But first of all you must hear my secret,' she said. With these words she took the prince by the hand and led him in silence into a shadowed hollow in the garden. There she bent down to two wild flowers. 'Do you hear what the Lily is telling

me? Do you understand the words of the Wormwood flower?' she asked and when the prince shook his head in puzzlement, she went on, 'The Lily flower is warning me. She is saying that the moment I put on my wedding gown, my time on earth will be over. And the Wormwood flower is whispering that the moment I put a wedding garland on my head, I shall return for ever to the kingdom of flowers. Forget me, I should not bring you good luck.'

The love-stricken prince would not be deterred, however, and when her royal parents added their voices to his entreaties, the princess at last consented to the wedding. Everyone in the kingdom was happy. People hugged each other with delight and swift messengers went out in all directions to invite the wedding guests. When the special day at last dawned and the maids-in-waiting were dressing Camomile in her wedding robes, the princess sighed with unhappiness and went as white as death. Rainbow tears gushed from her eyes. The tears changed into butterflies which settled into her golden hair like flowers. Hardly had the bridesmaids placed the wedding garland on her golden hair than the unfortunate Camomile dropped unconscious to the floor. The unhappy prince in tears took her in his arms and kissed her. Under his kisses, her body was transformed into a small delicate flower with a crown of white petals.

'Goodbye, my love,' the flower whispered. 'I am Camomile the daughter of the flowers. In gratitude for your love, there will always be enclosed within me a magical power that can ease human pain.'

When you are walking through the green meadow, one of the pathways might lead you to the forgotten kingdom. It is ruled over by the golden king and the silver queen and the diamond prince kneels at their throne. They are still as young and beautiful as at the beginning of time but their hearts are heavy with grief and sorrow as they think of the daughter they once had. The only comfort they gain is from a small delicate flower which grows in the meadow. It smells sweetly of love and bitter from sorrow. People call it Camomile.

How the Bee-herd almost became King

'It's my turn, it's my turn!' called a lively young girl with sweet-smelling bells on her cap. The Rose Queen stroked her kindly, saying, 'Do tell us a story, Princess Lily of the Valley, but I must tell you, don't make your story too sad!'

Once upon a time, beyond the blue stream and the green grove, stood a little village, as pretty as a picture. Quite near it, just a stone's throw away, was a poor little herdsman's hut with a thatched roof. In the summer the sun beat down on it, when it was wet the rain found its way in and from morning till night the wind played tunes for the mice to dance to. At that time, a poor little orphan, a tiny swineherd, lived in the hut. Because he wore a little hat with turned-up brim and jay's feather and a daisy tucked smartly into its ribbon, his neighbours called him just Little Tralala. Needless to say, roast chicken did not fly into his mouth after work and, as for pork, he might just about lick a bristle on festive days, but Little Tralala didn't complain.

'Thank God. What isn't today will be tomorrow,' he said to himself when the mean farmers did not cut him even a slice of dry bread to take

to pasture. He took up his willow stick and went off after the pigs with a merry song on his lips.

Once in the early morning, the little swineherd was sitting on the weir which crossed the stream. The sun was warm and his eyes were closing in peaceful sleep, when... oh my goodness! The little swineherd jumped up as though he had been stung by a wasp. Bother those pigs! They should be ashamed of themselves! They were contentedly rooting and joyfully squeaking as they stuffed themselves for all they were worth in the mayor's maize field.

The mayor had seen what was happening and came running out of his house. 'You wicked good-for-nothing, you lousy rascal, you swine prince,' he shouted until his paunch shook, 'let us not see you in the village any more as long as you live. Get out of my sight!'

What could poor Little Tralala do? He bundled together his few belongings and went. Where to? He followed his nose. Where else?

As he went along, there was a sudden booming and roaring in front of him and a storm blew up. Goodness gracious! A giant! 'Where are you off to, you little runt?' the giant snapped at the swineherd. Poor Tralala was shaking with fright. He soon came to his senses, however, and spoke. 'Who are you calling a little runt?' he said boldly.

'You, you little runt,' the giant chuckled.

'That's where you're mistaken, you are one big runt,' Little Tralala stood his ground. They stood there arguing who was the biggest runt and when they were tired of it the giant said, 'I see that you are brave. Why not come into my service? What can you do?'

'What can I do?' Little Tralala answered. 'I am a swineherd. I know how to herd swine.'

'Now that is just what I need,' said the giant, delighted. 'I'll take you to my meadow and you look after my shadows,' and he led the little swineherd to the meadow.

'But remember,' the giant said solemnly, 'don't let a single one escape otherwise you will be in trouble.'

That might be so, but the sun was shining with all its might and shadows were strewn over the meadow like daisies, from the birches, the firs, the pines and whatever else. Little Tralala broke off a fresh willow stick and settled comfortably under a fir tree. What was there for

him to do? He was minding the giant's shadows. Who wanted to argue about nothing with that foolish beanpole? All of a sudden, a cloud rolled up from somewhere, the sun hid behind it and, out of the blue, all the shadows were gone. The giant appeared in a twinkling.

'Where are my shadows?' he demanded to know.

'Where should they be?' Little Tralala answered, 'I sent them to drink at the forest spring. They already obey me at a word. When they have satisfied their thirst, I'll call them back,' he added watching the sky from the corner of his eye. The sun was about to reappear from behind the cloud. Little Tralala quickly whistled and, the moment the sun appeared, the shadows were once again dancing over the meadow. Little Tralala stayed in the meadow watching the shadows all day. As the evening drew near, he said to the giant, 'I've looked after your shadows long enough, pay me and I'll be getting along.'

The giant paid him well and Little Tralala went off. He went a whole night and a day and then another night and day until he reached a birch grove. Without warning, a dwarf appeared and stood in his path. His beard was so long that it touched the ground. 'Where are you off to, longlegs?' the dwarf piped.

'Longlegs yourself,' Little Tralala snapped. They argued a while as to who was the biggest longlegs until the dwarf said, 'I see you are not lost for words. Come and work for me. What can you do?'

'I am a swineherd, so that's what I do,' Little Tralala said.

'That suits me down to the ground. You can take my bees to pasture, but don't let a single one fly away or you will work for me without pay for the rest of your life.'

Little Tralala agreed and he had made a good bargain. The job was not tiring. As soon as the morning dew had dried up, he knocked on the hive, the bees swarmed out and scattered over the meadow flowers. As the sun set, they returned home of their own accord, and without exception, not one was missing. Little Tralala was content. One evening, however, heady scent found its way into the birch grove. 'What is it that smells so delightful?' Little Tralala asked.

'The Lily of the valley Kingdom is quite near here,' the dwarf answered. 'Its ruler is an old king. He has a daughter who is as beautiful as a meadow flower, but who is as changeable as the weather in Spring. Crowds of suitors come to the castle but the ones who cannot fulfil the task she sets them are beheaded without mercy.'

'I'm sure I'd get the better of her,' Little Tralala thought to himself and the scent of the lilies of the valley gave him a good idea.

'I'll take your bees to pasture in the Lily of the valley Kingdom,' he told the dwarf, 'you'll see that they will bring you sweet-smelling honey.'

The dwarf agreed and that very evening, Little Tralala took the hive with the sleeping bees on his back and set out. The next day he arrived in the Lily of the valley Kingdom. He perched his hat smartly on one side of his head and boldly hammered on the golden gate. 'I am the swineherd Little Tralala. I have come to marry the princess,' he called.

'Yet another unfortunate wretch,' the old king sighed, 'I can already picture him without his head.' Nevertheless, he ordered the little swineherd to be brought to the princess's chamber. All that splendour made Little Tralala dizzy. Wherever he stepped, his feet sank into a soft carpet which was woven of real lily of the valley blooms. The inconstant princess was stretched out on golden cushions, yawning with boredom and playing with a bouquet of lilies of the valley made from pure white gold. The flowers looked so real you could not tell the difference between them and the live lilies of the valley.

'So you want to marry me, you ragamuffin?' said the princess smiling in pity. 'As you like. If you fulfil the task I set you, I'll marry you. What is more, you will get half of the kingdom and a wedding cake to boot. Otherwise, you go to the executioner.'

Saying this, she ordered Little Tralala to turn

round. She then took up the golden bouquet and set it somewhere in the living carpet among the live flowers.

'Now, you poor ragamuffin, look for it!' she ordered. 'If you don't find my gold bouquet among the other flowers by evening, you will lose your head.'

Little Tralala turned round and as far as eye could see, there was nothing but lily of the valley flowers. The glowing green and white carpet spread throughout the palace, from the palace out into the garden, from the garden into the fields and from the fields to the mountains.

'If I lived a thousand years, I'd never find the princess's bouquet in this jungle of flowers,' he thought with horror. He felt sad and then he remembered his bees.

'My poor little bees. I forgot to let them out to graze. Get up, my little ladies, it's daytime already!' said the swineherd, banging on the hive. The bees swarmed out and scattered over the sweet-smelling flowers. The swineherd looked at them unhappily.

'How shall I look without my head?' he wondered. 'Where shall I put my smart hat? The bees did not know the answer. They flew from flower to flower and grazed contentedly. There was one spot however, where they did not land.

'That's it!' he cried, and ran to the flowers that the bees did not land on. He pulled them from the carpet and lo and behold, to his joy, he held the princess's bouquet in his hand. The wise bees were not deceived by the flowers of pure gold and so they helped the little swineherd to fulfil the impossible task.

When the princess caught sight of Little

Tralala with the golden bouquet in his hand, she scowled sullenly, but the old king set him on the throne and said, 'Take off your hat, Little Tralala, so that I can place the crown on your head. You will now be king.'

'Whoever saw a swineherd without his hat?' Little Tralala objected.

'Whoever saw a king without a crown?' the king insisted, but Little Tralala was stubborn. He pulled on his little hat and stuck out his tongue at the princess.

'If that's how it is, I am not interested in playing the king, or even in marrying your daughter, your majesty,' he said. And because the bees were already back from the pasture, he took the hive on his back and without saying goodbye, set off back to see the dwarf. Indeed, the dwarf was waiting impatiently for him. Perhaps he is still grazing the dwarf's bees in the birch grove. Perhaps he has married a forest nymph. Who knows? Ask any wandering bee, he might tell you.

'It can't be helped,' sighed the Lily of the valley princess in the end. 'That little hat, turned up on both sides and with a jay's feather and a daisy tucked into the snakeskin hat band, suited him best of all — far better than any king's golden crown.'

The Queen of the Night

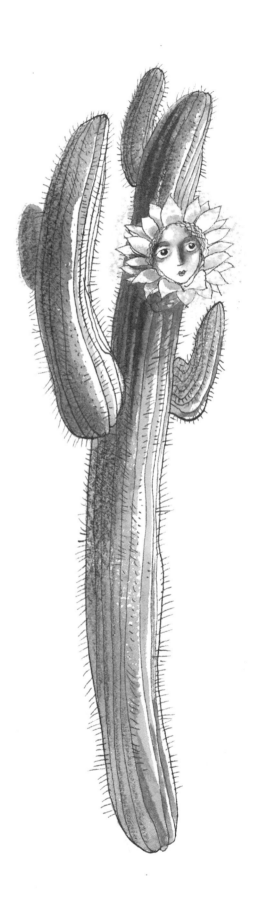

It was nearly midnight. The pale light of the stars poured down from the sky and swarms of fireflies hovered over the dancing flowers. All at once, a hush came over the Rose Queen's garden and a moonbeam shone on a forlorn cactus plant in the darkest corner. As if by magic, a bud unfolded on his thorny stem and turned into a splendid silvery-white flower in a golden calyx. From out of the flower stepped a lovely girl. 'Welcome, little sister,' said the Rose Queen. 'Welcome to you, Queen of the Night. Are you bringing us a fairytale?' The graceful girl nodded silently and in a soft voice began to tell her story.

Far, far away, over the hills and across many seas, lies a magic land. In the heart of this country there is a vast desert. In the middle of the desert there once stood a palace of darkness which appeared by night, lit up by countless stars, but every morning with the first rays of the sun, it disappeared like the shadows of night. A kindly Queen, who was also young and beautiful, lived in the palace. As soon as the moon gave its signal to the evening dusk, the queen took her place on her golden throne, combed out her black hair and spread it over the whole region. She then called her two sisters, the Princess of Sweet Dreams and the Princess of Nightmares.

'Fly, dear sisters, out into the wide world and do your work. I entrust to your care the people of the earth. Take your place near the heads of those who are sleeping and read to them from the books of dreams, the wonderful tales of the Queen of the Night. Princess of Sweet Dreams, I ask you to settle silenty near the pillow of the handsome young man in the palm grove and tell him about me in your nicest dream. I have locked his eyelids with the silver key of sleep and covered his face with my raven-black hair many times. He appeals to me and I would like him to become my husband.'

After these words, the sisters flew out into the world like evening breezes. Wherever the Princess of Nightmares entered the homes of people, there came cries of distress and the weeping of children who had woken in the night. The face of the Princess was ugly and her stories aroused terror, but the kindly Princess of Sweet Dreams comforted the frightened sleepers with soothing words. She was often reproached for this by her ungracious sister who would say, 'It is not my fault, sister, that at birth I was given only the gift of ugliness and evil. I cannot help it if, deep in my heart, I am jealous of the Queen of the Night. When my time comes, I shall get my revenge.'

'My poor sister,' the Princess of Sweet Dreams said with regret. 'It must be terrible to live with envy in your heart.'

At last there came a night when the Princess of Sweet Dreams noticed a humble little hut in a palm grove on her nightly wandering. Down from the sky she dropped, settling at the head of a handsome young man. She covered his face with her hair and began to tell him a story. That night the young man dreamed of a beautiful queen in a palace of stars in the middle of a desert.

'Whoever kisses the Queen of the Night with the first ray of the sun will become her husband for ever after,' the Princess of Sweet Dreams whispered and the young man smiled happily in his sleep. All at once, the ugly face of the Princess of Nightmares appeared near the sleeper's head.

'Your beautiful dream will not come true,' the ugly creature croaked. 'When the time comes, I, the Princess of Nightmares, will gain power over the Queen of the Night and you will help me to do so. I will turn her into a frightful, thorny plant with the body of a snake. Everyone who sees it will turn away in disgust.'

Just then, the sky paled with the dawn and the first ray of the sun sent away the shadows of the night. The young man awoke with tears in his eyes, but the morning sun soon swept away the memory of his bad dreams. From that time, wherever he went, the young man could think of no one else but the Queen of the Night.

One day he said to his parents, 'Somewhere in the middle of the desert is a palace woven of darkness and there my bride is waiting for me. I am going to look for her.'

'The desert is endless, my son, anyone who gets lost there meets his death,' his father warned, but his mother smiled lovingly and gave him her blessing.

'Go, my son,' she said, 'for love is greater than death and to die in search of love is better than never to love at all.'

from the fire at the last moment. Gently he blew on the burned wings.

'Thank you,' said the moth gratefully. 'I know you are seeking the palace of the Queen of the Night. I shall help you find it. Listen to me carefully! When you put out your fire, in which I burned my wings, swallow the last spark. You will change into a night moth and you will be able to smell all the different scents of far away flowers. There will be one which takes your senses above all the others — the sweet vanilla perfume of the Queen of the Night. Follow that one. When you arrive at the star palace, silently settle at the Queen's feet, but do not try to kiss her before the first ray of the sun appears on the horizon.' With this the moth flew away.

The young man did not waste a moment. As soon as the flames died down, he swallowed the last spark from the hot ash. It burned his mouth, but to his great joy, straight away he turned into a little night moth. Suddenly he was able to smell all the different scents of far away flowers. He set out on the trail of the sweetest of all. He flew and flew until he saw a wonderful palace shining with rainbow-coloured stars. The moon glowed on its highest tower. At last he had reached his goal!

The Queen of the Night was sitting on her golden throne with her hair let down and stars shone in the depths of her eyes. When the night moth silently settled at her feet and changed once again into a handsome young man, the queen smiled happily.

'Is it you, my love?' she whispered. At that, the young man could not resist and he threw his arms around her and kissed her lips. In a flash, all the stars were put out and the ugly laughter of the Princess of Nightmares echoed through the room.

'You fool!' she cried, 'you did not wait with

So the brave young man set out into the desert to seek his fortune. More dead than alive, he sought in vain through endless days in the hot desert. The sun burned his eyes and to avoid dying of thirst, he drank his own tears. One evening when his strength had all but left him, he made a fire from the dried stems of cactuses, rolled himself into a ball and cried in despair.

Just then a little night moth circled over the fire and, attracted by the light, fell helplessly into the flames. The young man snatched her

your kiss for sunrise and so you have put the queen in my power. Woe betide you, sister! Woe betide you, you proud Queen of the Night! It is my wish that you turn into an ugly, thorny cactus from which people will turn away with disgust!'; and so it happened.

Then the Princess of Sweet Dreams, appeared wearing a scorched dress. 'Why did you not obey me?' she asked sadly. 'I cannot undo the harm my wicked sister has done, but I can change it. One year from this day, a lovely flower will bloom on the ugly snake-like body of the Queen of the Night and will entice the night moth with its delicate scent. It will bloom for one night only. If her lover does not come, she will die with the first ray of the sun.'

At that moment, the dawn broke on the horizon and the star palace dissolved as if with the wave of a magic wand. The unhappy young man woke up in his little hut with tears in his eyes.

'Was it only a dream?' he said to himself, but then he felt a sting in his palm, and there he found three long, sharp thorns – the last souvenir of the Queen of the Night.

Day followed day, but time did not lessen the young man's sorrow. Then one evening he was blessed with peaceful sleep, and the Princess of Sweet Dreams silently settled near his head. 'If you have the courage to seek your lost love,' she whispered, 'swallow a thorn of the Queen of the Night. You will turn into a night moth which can sense all the fragrances of far away flowers. Woe betide you, if you don't find her. You will remain bewitched as a night moth of the desert forever.'

The young man woke from his sleep. He did not hesitate and did as his dream had told him to do. Instantly he changed into a night moth and flew longingly towards the sweetest fragrance. However, the Princess of Nightmares had been listening to her sister and wasting no time had scattered grains of desert sand in many places, all over the earth. Wherever a grain fell, the snake body of the ugly cactus took root within a moment. There were thousands and thousands of them and on each one bloomed a lovely flower, smelling sweetly like the raven hair of the Queen of the Night. The unhappy night moth wanders from flower to flower but has not yet found the real Queen of the Night. Perhaps even now, he is still looking for his long-lost love.

From that time, all over the world, year after year, countless flowers bloom. With their delicate perfume, they lure the cicadas and the night moths, but if their lovers do not come, they die with the first ray of the morning sun.

Each year, for a single night, the Queen of the Night blooms lost among the thousands of other flowers.

Thus the Queen of the Night ended her story in the garden of the Rose Queen. The sky paled and there was a shy red glow over the horizon.

'My night moth did not come,' she said with a sad smile. 'My time has come. When the first ray of the sun shines, I shall die.' At that very moment, a little night moth hovered above her head and silently settled at her feet. With that, he changed into a handsome young man and gently kissed the Queen of the Night. Soft music played and the young man and the Queen of the Night danced together in a happy embrace until they dissolved in the first rays of the sun.

Mary Dogrose

In the Rose Queen's garden, one of the girls was dancing more wildly than the others. She was laughing loudly and her long hair billowed around her head like an extravagant cloud. Into it was woven a crown of dogroses. 'My dear Dogrose,' the Rose Queen entreated, 'please tell us your story.' Everyone listened with bated breath.

Once upon a time there was a king who liked best of all to rule his kingdom from his bed.

That little bed had hangings made of the finest golden cobwebs and was overgrown with wild roses. It looked like a dogrose bush in full bloom. One fine day the lazy king had an idea.

'I shall get married,' he told his counsellors. 'I shall marry the first woman who can jump straight over my royal bedstead, and in doing so, she must not touch a single thorn or knock off a single bud. That is my royal word.'

He gave orders at once for himself and his

bed to be carried to the square of the royal town. When the news spread, marriage-hungry girls hurried there for all they were worth. Beautiful ones and ugly ones, small and tall, brunettes and blondes, black-eyed and blue-eyed girls. There was great confusion in the town square and so much noise!

The first jumped, then the second and third – every girl had a turn. One tore her skirt, another got a thorn in her leg, that one lost her underslip, this one almost got herself killed but not one of them could jump over the bed. Just then, a poor widow came into the square. Not young, not old, just about right, as the saying goes. The king could not take his eyes off her.

'Jump, young lady, what are you waiting for?' he cried.

The widow did not wait to be asked a second time. She lifted her skirt, hop, skip and jump, and was over the bed like a feather. Even so, her foot just touched the highest bud and it rolled down to the ground, but the clever little widow nimbly gathered it up as she flew through the air, and, so that the king would not see, she quickly swallowed it.

'Goodness, gracious me, now that is a woman to my taste,' the king rejoiced, 'she will jump according to how I whistle.' She did not jump, however. Before the king could wipe the tears of laughter from his eyes, the handsome widow had disappeared as though the earth had swallowed her up. While the king's messengers searched for her far and wide, she was living as before in her little cottage on the outskirts of the town. And what do you think? Before a year had passed, she gave birth to a little flower bud, the second year she was a lovely little girl and the third year a grown-up young woman, beautiful as her fairytale mother. The widow called her Mary Dogrose because her hair was the colour of roses.

When her hair had grown long enough to touch the ground, her mother sent her into the town to learn to embroider. All day long Mary Dogrose sat with the other students under the lime tree in the town square and stitched and stitched. Can you guess what she embroidered? Nothing but rose buds. Whoever bought a little white handkerchief from her found that the bud opened out into a fragrant little rose.

Meanwhile, the king was beside himself with worry, he longed so much for the fine widow. When his yearning drove him out of the palace, he ordered seven pairs of royal white horses to be harnessed to the royal bed and set out in search of her. He drove on steadily, snuggled into his cushions, staring here and there to see what was going on, when suddenly he came across a group of merry young women under the old lime tree. The loveliest of all was Mary Dogrose. They were stitching away, embroidering, chattering and gossiping, never silent a moment. The king could not take his eyes off them, especially Mary Dogrose. He started chatting to them, and because he enjoyed their talk, he promised to come again and bring each of them a golden stool.

Mary Dogrose arrived home in a very cheer-ful mood. At once she confided in her mother how she looked forward to the king's gift, but her mother gave her this advice. 'You must accept nothing from the king, I will give you a little golden stool myself, one that everyone else will envy, and when the king asks who you are and where you live, tell him this,' and she whispered something in Mary's ear.

The next day the king came with his gifts of golden stools for all the girls. Only Mary Dogrose refused his gift. She showed him the stool her mother had given her. It was much more beautiful than the one from the king.

'Who are you and where do you live?' the king asked angrily.

'I am Mary Dogrose
And my dear mother is Rose,
Dogrose bush my father,
We live, because we'd rather,
In a cottage of rosy shade
Set in a Dogrose glade.'

Such was the answer of Mary Dogrose. The king was not much pleased with this reply, but conversing with so many charming young girls put him in a better mood.

He promised that the next time he would bring each of them a golden cushion, but Mary Dogrose got an even more beautiful cushion from her mother and refused the one from the king. So it went on, with golden thread, golden thimbles and golden fringes for their embroidery. Mary already had them all and took nothing from the king. One day the king brought golden needlecases for the girls, but this time too, Mary could not be persuaded. The king could not control his anger.

'How dare you refuse the royal gifts?' he thundered. 'Here you are!' and he threw the golden needlecase at Mary's head.

Ouch, that was bad luck! You can't imagine how painful it was when Mary Dogrose combed her rose-coloured hair to remove the golden needles! It took her the whole day and even then, she left one little needle in. When she walked home in the evening, crying, she met a strange old woman with three snake eyes and three lizard tongues. She was a witch. 'Where are you off to, young lady, with that needle in your hair? Wait a minute. I'll take it out for you,' said the old hag sweetly.

Obediently, Mary bent her head, but the old witch drove the needle deep on to the nape of her neck. At that moment Mary Dogrose turned into a pink dove. She flew into the air,

circled round and without knowing why, flew off to the royal palace. There the unhappy bird settled on a Dogrose branch near the king's bed. The king was surprised but because the little dove was so tame and gentle, he soon became very fond of her. The little dove did not move an inch from his bed.

One day the king was speaking to his counsellors. 'It is not very likely I'll ever find the lovely widow,' he said. 'I have decided to sail to the Isle of Beautiful Women to look for another bride there.'

He ordered his bed to be taken to the harbour and let down on to the water. He had seven pairs of white fish harnessed to it and seven pairs of white sails set above it and gave the command to sail on the high seas, but the boat did not move from the pier.

'Have you forgotten something, your majesty?' his counsellors asked. With that, the king snapped his fingers and immediately sent a messenger to the palace to ask his dear little dove what he should bring her from his long journey. The little dove replied.

'The stone teardrop I ask you, please,
From which is flowing peaceful ease,
And the flower that from the wild fern springs
And to the needful sweet death brings.'

The messenger had only just given the king this message when the wind blew and the bed sailed out on to the high seas as swiftly as an arrow. They sailed and sailed until they arrived at the Isle of Beautiful Women, but none of the lovely creatures took the king's fancy. So he gave orders to sail to the Isle of Even-More-Beautiful Women.

'If I am not suited here either, then I'll make for home without delay. I am already missing my dear little dove,' the king said sadly. The king was not suited. Beauties there were, real pictures to gladden the eye, but the king could not find one among them to love. Saddened, he gave the command to return home, but no matter what they did, the bed would not budge from the harbour.

'Have you forgotten something?' his counsel-

her lost love. Alongside grows a green fern with a single white flower. Take it to your rosy dove.'

Hearing this, the king at once gave orders for the bed, with him on it, to be pulled ashore and because they had no horses in that land, he had seven pairs of white mice harnessed to the bed. The bed, however, would not move an inch. Like it or not, the king had to leave his comfortable cushions and set out on foot. Surprisingly, he quite enjoyed that search and did not pine even once for his royal bed. When, after a long struggle, he at last climbed to the top of the high mountain, he found everything as the old beggar woman had told him. He tied up the stone teardrop in a scarf, stuck the fern flower into his hair and returned merrily to the coast. Then he raced the wind on the shortest journey home.

When the king greeted his little pink dove back at the palace and handed her his gifts, it seemed to him that a smile flickered across the little bird's face. On his return, he no longer wanted to lie about lazily in his bed. He wandered on his own throughout the meadows and forests, enjoyed himself hunting and made little boats of tree bark and grass stalks to send down the stream to the sea. He could not rid himself of a strange sadness which seemed to have overcome him. Once he returned home unexpectedly from his wandering and heard a quiet, sorrowful voice speaking these words.

'Dear little teardrop of stone,
Please do not let me pine alone,
Oh fern flower, with your fragrant breath
Ease my pain or take me in forgetful death.'

The king looked around but saw no one besides his dear little pink dove. He took her in his hand and gently ruffled her feathers. There

lors asked the king. It was then the ruler remembered the wish of his little dove. 'Wherever shall I find a stone teardrop? Where shall I go to find a fern flower? Who ever heard of a fern that blossomed?' he cried, racking his brains. Just then, an old beggar woman called from the harbour, asking for alms. The king threw her a gold coin and added to it a rose bud from his bed. The beggar woman thanked him, saying, 'You have done well by not refusing me. I will advise you, where to find what you are looking for. In the centre of the island stands a high mountain. At the top of this mountain are the stone tears of a young girl who cried for was something shining among them. It was a little golden needle. He quickly drew it out of the little dove's neck. In that moment, Mary Dogrose, more beautiful than ever, stood before him thanking him wholeheartedly for releasing her. She then told the king everything about herself and her mother. The king wasted no time. He took Mary Dogrose by the hand and they set off together for the rose-coloured cottage on the rose-coloured hill, but it was not Mary's mother they found there. Instead, there was a pink dove sitting by the fireside. She seemed to be smiling. Then she spoke with a human voice.

'You two must now live for each other and I must fly away.'

'Where to?' Mary Dogrose whispered.

'To Heaven,' the dove replied and rose up to the clouds.

So the king married Mary Dogrose and if they have not died, they will be living happily to this day. What happened to the royal flower bed? Why, a little baby was born in it — rosy and fragrant, just like a rose bud.

A Bell for a Tomcat

A pair of flowery lovers nestled close to each other in a cut-glass vase. A handsome youth rang his bright blue bell while a girl replied with her shining white bell. They chattered together and asked each other riddles.

'Guess, if you can, what I am thinking now,' the young girl teased.

'The mice in the pantry are making such a row,' the young man replied and carried straight on.

The mice were having a ball and all the important mice were there. No one could remember such an occasion before. To this day, they are still talking about it – ask any mouse! Fashionable young mice in velvet jackets, girls in fur coats like ermine, sleek rats with bristling whiskers – they were all eating and drinking, making merry, dancing and romping till their tails were all shaky. When the celebrations were at their height, who should turn up but the velvet-pawed tomcat? He crouched ready to pounce, his green eyes lit up and – oops! – he had a mouse in his claws. As for the others, it was as though a gun had been fired in their midst. Wherever there was a hole, they were into it.

They huddled there without a sound, shaking with fear and anguish. After some time, however, they felt the pangs of hunger. The mouse elder called them all together in the little underground passage.

'Not one of you now dares to stick his nose

outside the hole,' that wise fellow said. 'If we do not get the better of the tomcat, we will either end up in his tummy or we'll die of hunger. Let's put our heads together and decide what we should do.'

Well, as for good advice, there's precious little of it about. The mice racked their brains but could not come up with anything, until one old mouse granny cried, 'I've got it, my dears! Let us gather together all our riches and we'll get the bell founder to cast us a nice little bell. We'll hang that bell round the tomcat's neck and the next time he comes creeping towards us, the little bell will tinkle and we can all run away in time. We'll get the better of that light-pawed one!'

All the mice cheered and at once set to work. They harnessed twelve pairs of white mice to an old tablespoon and on to the spoon they loaded all their treasures — a piece of cheese, an oat ear, the sole of a shoe, a piece of bacon rind, a tallow candle, a crust of bread and other goodies with which to pay the bell founder. Off they went through secret passages to the bell founder's workshop. The bell founder threw up his hands at such a questionable pile of goodies, but he was a kind man and did not turn the mice away. He smelted and blew his bellows, and finally cast the little bell. A beauty! It tinkled like the bell on a jester's cap.

'What colour shall I make it?' the bell founder asked. The mice agreed on blue because blue would look very handsome on the black cat. So the bell founder tempered the bell to a fine blue colour and the mice set out happily on their way home.

'So we've won through!' they all cried. 'The cat won't surprise us anymore. Now all we have to do is hang the bell on his neck.'

Oh dear, you fellows! Who will hang that

little bell on the tomcat's neck? The mice looked at each other, hardly breathing. What now? The mouse granny had another idea.

'Let the bravest of you do it.'

'What sort of idea is that?' objected the mouse who was always boasting about his courage. 'Why, I am even scared of my own tail. Send the strongest of us to the tomcat.'

'You think I am the strongest?' the toughest mouse of all said angrily. 'Indeed, I can't even bend a mouse's whisker. My own wife at home beats me. Let the cleverest of us tie the bell on the tomcat.'

'Not on your life!' fumed the most cunning mouse. 'In all my life I've never done anything you might call clever. I can't tell my right foot from my left or decide what's cheese and what's bacon fat. Let us send the stupidest of us to the tomcat,' but not one of the mice was stupid enough to tackle the soft-pawed tomcat.

So, in the end, the mice scattered in all directions and they threw the bell out into the fields. There it was found by a little flower fairy who hung it on a bare flower stem, set it ringing merrily and went about her business.

'So now you know how we, the flowers of the meadow, came to have our lovely little bells,' said the harebell, bowing elegantly and tinkling his little bell softly. Ting-a-ling-a-ling went the little bell to show that it was the end of the story.

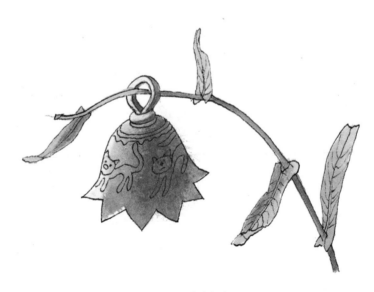

The Goose-girl

The next to tell her tale was a girl wearing a short skirt of little lilac flowers.

'There was once a little water nymph who was called Syrinx and she was turned into a reed,' she began.

'And what happened?' the Rose Queen asked.

'I've forgotten how it goes on,' the little girl sighed and started to cry.

'It doesn't matter,' the queen said kindly, 'you'll think of another story,' and she did. This is how it goes.

There was once a lilac bush, and he had a sister, a branch of lilac. They grew close together near the path at the foot of a hill. The path ran from one place to another and back again. It was used by fairies. When a mild, Maytime night blanketed the countryside, the lilac bush turned into a merry shepherd who blew on his little elder-wood whistle and – hop skip and jump – a little fairy leaped down from the lilac branch. The shepherd played and played, the fairy danced and the whole countryside smelled so sweet that the lovers in the meadows were giddy with it. Then, when

morning came, the shepherd and the fairy took on their flower likeness once again.

One evening, a poor goose-girl came to this place. She curled up under the little lilac bush, took the goose and her goslings on to her lap and burst out crying.

'What are you crying for?' a kind voice asked. Standing before her she saw a shepherd wearing a white smock and holding an elder-wood whistle.

'Oh dear, I am unhappy because I am all alone in the world,' the girl answered. 'My wicked stepmother and my stepsister have chased me from my home and my father hadn't the courage to stop them. I've nowhere even to lie down and go to sleep.'

The shepherd boy smiled, blew on his whistle and a beautiful fairy dressed in a skirt of lilac flowers appeared.

'Come and dance with me and you'll see that your unhappiness will pass,' she entreated the goose-girl. With that, the shepherd boy whistled a merry tune, the fairy took the girl by the hand and they danced until they could dance no more. Even the goose and her goslings joined in. So much happy laughter! At last the young girl rolled into the grass breathless.

'That's enough,' she laughed, 'my feet are aching and I cannot keep my eyes open any longer.'

'Yes, it's time to go to sleep,' the young shepherd said, 'but before we say goodbye, take this elder-wood whistle as a present. You will find out that it is magic. When you blow it, all the flowers will start dancing and whatever you wish will be granted.'

'And I will give you my little skirt,' the fairy added. 'The moment you twirl it around, the wind will carry you off wherever you want to go,' but the little goose girl hardly heard the fairy's words, for she was already asleep. She did not wake until the sun was high in the sky.

'Oh, that was a beautiful dream,' she sighed,

'But what is this?' Beside her, on the grass, lay an elder-wood whistle and a little skirt of lilac flowers. The girl put it on, twirled around and immediately she was flying over hills and dales, wherever she wanted. Wherever she travelled, she blew merry little songs on the whistle. All the flowers opened up as soon as they heard the music and in each one lay a new secret. The young girl played to a white rose and out of the rose stepped a white girl who bowed to her three times and danced three times. She played to a blue-eyed forget-me-not from out of which leaped a young knight in blue armour who swung his sword three times and three times saluted with it on all sides. She played to a golden dandelion and out of it slipped laughing little princesses, who opened up their white umbrellas and flew far away.

So the gentle little goose-girl wandered the world and wherever she paused, she spread laughter and joy. She was no longer sad and everybody loved her, but the day came when she felt a longing for her home and most of all for her father. Wasting no time, she twirled the little skirt and before she knew it she was sitting with her geese in her arms at the side of their pond, right by the cottage she was born in. She let the goose and her goslings swim in the pond as she gazed in the cottage window.

Just then, her stepmother and stepsister ran out of the cottage.

'Off with you where you came from, you good-for-nothing! How dare you let your geese swim in our pond!' They began to shout louder and louder, and then started throwing stones at the poor geese. They would have killed all the little goslings if the mother goose had not sheltered them under her wings, but even so, the poor things were bleeding. The little goose-girl cried bitterly at such cruelty.

'I wish you would all turn into geese, you shameful creatures, so that you would know for yourself what such pain feels like,' she thought to herself, and to ease her pain, she blew on her whistle. As she blew, wonder of wonders, her stepmother and stepsister turned into geese, not beautiful like her own, but ugly with ruffled feathers. They cackled unhappily and waddled to the pond. All the boys from the village gathered at that moment as though they had been summoned and began throwing stones at the geese until feathers flew in all directions. Just then, the goose-girl's father came to the cottage door.

'It serves you right, you wretches,' he shouted at the geese. 'Why, miserable fellow that I am,

did I not stand up for my little daughter against you? Why did I allow you to chase her from her home? If only she could forgive me!' he lamented.

The little goose-girl turned to him and stroked his white hair. 'Don't you recognize me, father? I stopped being angry with you a long time ago,' she said. Her happy father, tears in his eyes, took her into his arms and led her and her geese into their little home. They lived there happily. As for the evil geese, they did not get off lightly. The village boys gave them no peace and the dogs of the town chased them up and down the main street until their little legs were nearly dropping off. The poor creatures, hardly managed to jump into the pond and even then, their troubles were not over.

Living on a farm in that village was a mad serving girl. She made up her mind that she wanted to get some feathers for a pillow. So she hid behind a bush near the pond and when the unfortunate geese came close to the edge, she grabbed them by the neck and because there was little sense in her head, started plucking them while they were still alive. You should have heard how those geese cackled, they were in such pain, and before you could say Jack Robinson, they were plucked bare. Not only that, but she had hardly pulled out the last quill when you could have knocked her down with a feather! Standing before her were the step-mother and her daughter, both as bald as a coot. Goodness me, what an uproar that caused in the village. The two bald women took to their heels and ran as far away as they could and never came back. So the goose-girl and her father and their geese lived in the cottage alone and were very happy.

The Story of the Banana Flower

'There was once an old monkey — perhaps more than just old — he might even have been the oldest monkey in the world. He was called all sorts of names. This or that, or maybe even Whatsit. Yes, for all I care, he could be called Whatsit, not a bad name after all. What do you say?' the lad who dwelled in the banana flower asked cheekily. 'The main thing is that I heard from him no end of stories. The monkey Whatsit was never short of a tale. He scratched behind his ear, that's were monkey stories are born, and snap! There was one in his fingers.'

This is thc talc thc chccky young lad from the banana flower told. Listen.

When Whatsit was just a little lad, there were still green monkeys in the world. You can thank the good spirits of the jungle that you never meet with such creatures nowadays. They were the most evil-minded and most artful creatures under the sun. They never did anyone any good, they pushed their inquisitive noses into everything and were delighted whenever they could do anyone an ill turn. Those monkeys did not even have their own proper names, every single one was called NdokengNdoke.

Then one day one of these green Ndo-kengNdoke met the old tortoise Kolokolo-pua. Of course, tortoises are naturally wise but they are rather too trusting. It could be because they have nothing to be afraid of. Instead of fur, they have on their backs a hard smooth shell on which many a greedy forest glutton has broken his teeth. So that tortoise Kolokolopua quite cordially and quite trustingly greeted the green monkey and asked her very politely where she was going.

'What business is it of yours?' Ndokeng-Ndoke snapped and gazed at the tortoise curiously. Then an idea was born in her malicious mind.

'Because it is you who ask, sister Kolokolopua, I'll tell you. I'm just going down to the river. It rained so much yesterday that the streams have flooded and lots of uprooted trees are floating down the river. I'll catch some wood and perhaps build a raft. Or it could be a big nest like the birds have. It is good for all sorts of things. If you like, I'll take you with me.'

Kolokolopua was glad that she would have something to do and enjoy for that day and agreed gladly. When they reached the river, a huge banana bush was just floating by.

'Hurry, Kolokolopua, you big lazy bones!' shouted the green monkey. Jump into the water before that bush floats away. Can't you see that sweet banana shining among the leaves?'

Feeling as though she had no choice, for as you remember she was a trusting soul, Kolokolopua threw herself into the stream and while she struggled with the banana bush, the green NdokengNdoke lounged on the bank and shouted to the tortoise to hurry up. When Kolokolopua finally floundered to the bank, NdokengNdoke shouted, 'Hand that banana bush to me, I'll help you pull it out. Never in my life have I seen anyone so clumsy. You must want me to do everything myself!'

The tired tortoise obeyed, but NdokengNdoke at once grabbed the sweet banana, shoved it into her mouth and again left the tortoise to fend for herself.

'What are you doing?' Kolokolopua cried angrily, 'you promised that we would share everything equally.'

'I had to try the banana to see if it was ripe,' NdokengNdoke laughed. 'Now I know, but unfortunately, there is none left for you, I am very sorry. Wait until new ones grow on the branches for us. To show you how just I am, I'll share fairly with you. You take the roots and I'll take the top.'

The tortoise agreed. She took the roots and planted them in the ground. The green monkey did the same. She planted the branches of banana leaves in the ground.

'Oh, you stupid tortoise,' she thought to

herself, 'don't you know that bananas grow on the branches and not on the roots? I shall be interested to see what sort of harvest you get.'

Days passed and the monkey Ndokeng-Ndoke greedily examined her banana branches. The leaves were beginning to turn yellow, to wither. 'They are getting ripe.' The monkey was delighted when she saw the yellow leaves which were the same colour as ripe bananas. Before long, however, the leaves fell off and the monkey was left with bare branches. In a bad mood she went off to visit the tortoise Kolokolopua.

'Have you got bananas on your roots yet?' she teased the tortoise, but then she flew into a temper. A slim trunk had risen up from the banana tree's roots and from it had grown first one leaf and then another and third until a little green bush glowed under the blue sky. Flowers had bloomed among the leaves, they had opened, and in their place had grown juicy fruits. The branches were bending under their weight. NdokengNdoke was almost beside herself with rage.

When the bananas were ripe, the trusting tortoise asked the envious monkey to do her a favour. 'My dear sister NdokengNdoke, please do an honest job for me. I cannot climb trees like you. Please be so good as to climb up and pick the bananas for me. I will share my crop with you. You can have every second banana you pick.'

NdokengNdoke wasted no time. She was in the branches in a trice. She picked the smallest banana and threw it down to the tortoise Kolokolopua.

'The first!' she cried and at once crammed the second into her mouth. In no time she was greedily biting into the third banana.

'Hey, what are you doing?' the tortoise cried

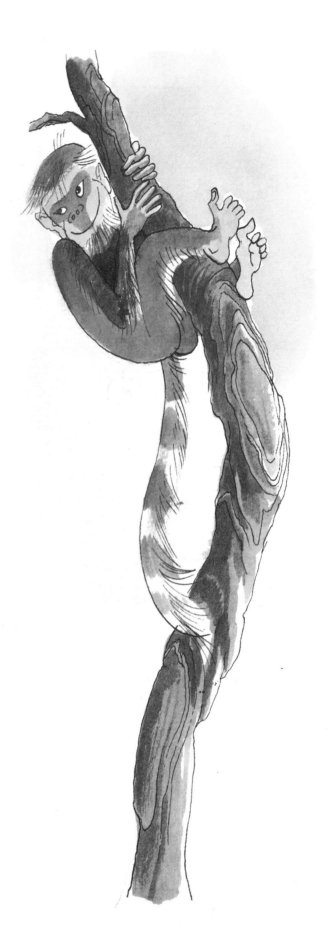

angrily. 'That banana belongs to me! Didn't I say that you could have every second banana?'

'And isn't it the second after the one before it?' the monkey laughed, and gulped down the fourth banana.

'Hold on,' Kolokolopua exhorted her. 'That one certainly doesn't belong to you. I must get every first banana after each of your second bananas.'

'That's where you make a big mistake,' NdokengNdoke said sharply with her mouth full, 'that is no first banana, that is by chance the fourth banana and, if I am not mistaken, it is also the second after the one before. You certainly got the very first one and I don't see any other first bananas here. There are only those that come after. Or do you want to call me a liar, to say that I am cheating you? That would be very thankless of you!' laughed the wicked wily monkey.

All this counting made the tortoise Kolokolopua dizzy. While she was carefully putting everything in order in her head, the monkey ate all the bananas and was gone.

'Well, look at that,' Kolokolopua thought sadly, 'I have lived in the world so long but I have not yet learned the way monkeys count.'

Some time later, the tortoise was taking a walk in the jungle. Hanging from a tree in a rattan thicket was a loop of lovely green liana. It had been set there by hunters who wanted to catch an animal in it. It was a wonder that Kolokolopua herself did not get caught up in it. Standing there in front of the snare she thought how lucky she had been to miss it. Then in the tree above she heard a honey-sweet voice.

'What have you got there that is so interesting, sister Kolokolopua?' the green monkey whined. It was the same one who had cheated the tortoise out of her bananas. Kolokolopua

peered up at her and answered good-naturedly, 'Now what might it be? I have found a lovely emerald necklace in the thicket. I was just going to try it on to see how it would suit me.'

'Show me, show me!' cried the envious monkey. 'I'll try it first before you break it with your scaly head. Whoever saw a tortoise wearing a beautiful necklace?' and before you could blink the grasping monkey had pushed her head into the noose. With this, the supple tree, to which the vine was tied, sprang back and the monkey NdokengNdoke was strangled in the noose.

'The emerald necklace really suits you, poor NdokengNdoke,' the tortoise Kolokolopua sighed and a tear fell from her eye, because tortoises sometimes weep even when they don't feel like it. That's how tortoises are.

'So that is the story I heard from the old monkey Whatsit,' said the young man from the banana flower and he bowed respectfully to the Rose Queen.

Snowdrop

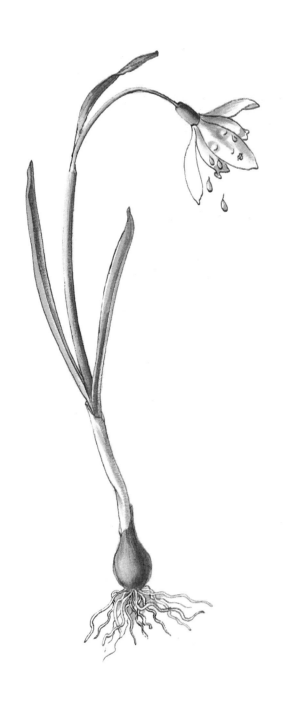

'Are you crying?' asked the Rose Queen, bending down to little Snowdrop.

'Oh no, I just feel tearful,' Snowdrop replied.

'And why do you feel tearful?' said the Queen.

'Because I am sad,' said the Snowdrop.

'Why are you sad?' asked the Queen.

'Because I am sad,' Snowdrop repeated stubbornly.

The Rose Queen sighed. 'Why don't you tell us one of your snowy tales. That might cheer you up.' So this is the tale she told.

There was once a young girl called Snowdrop because she wore a white apron and white clogs and had hair that was white like the fluff of a dandelion. Snowdrop's parents had died long ago and a mean farm woman had taken her in.

'Like that, I'll have a nimble little servant to help me,' said that greedy woman to herself rubbing her hands in glee. 'Why should I throw money away for nothing?' Well, Snowdrop had a horrid time with this woman. She was on the go from sun up to sun down, hardly able to stand on her feet for tiredness. On top of it all, the mean farm woman begrudged her every mouthful of food, and so the poor girl often went off to her bed hungry. How she cried into her pillow and how she missed her father and mother!

Once, in the winter, the farm woman was preparing for a ball. She was as vain as she was mean. All day long she preened in front of the mirror, trying on this and that, changing her skirt and her blouses, and was still not satisfied with her appearance. Snowdrop was kept running to and fro. Whatever she did she could not please the vain peacock. When she could hardly see for hunger, she noticed a crumb under the table. Snowdrop quickly swallowed it, hoping her mistress did not see her. But alas, the stingy woman saw her in the mirror and shouted at once, 'So that is how you behave, you ungrateful wretch! You want to eat my bread behind my back? That's what I get for taking you under my roof! That's the gratitude I get!' she grumbled. 'But let me tell you, if you don't bring me fresh flowers from the meadow for a garland by evening, you'll leave my house.'

Snowdrop implored her, but with no success. 'Wherever would I find fresh flowers, in the middle of winter?' she complained, but the farm woman would not let her off. What could the girl do? She put on her ragged apron and her white clogs and went where her feet carried her. The snow was so deep that it was up to her knees and the frost was so cold that no one dared go out. In no time, Snowdrop's teeth were chattering with cold like a rattle from the fair. As she dragged herself along, she saw a shrivelled old woman sitting in the snow. She was white, white as hoar frost. The poor thing was trembling like a leaf. 'God be with you, granny,' Snowdrop greeted her and because she

had a good heart, she untied her apron and threw it over the old woman's shoulders to warm her up a little, even though her own hands were numb with cold.

'Thank you, little girl,' the poor woman murmured, 'what are you doing out in such bad weather?' In tears, Snowdrop told her everything.

'Don't cry, don't be upset,' the old woman said comfortingly. 'We'll work something out together.' With that she drew from her pocket a little jacket made of moss. 'Put this on,' she told Snowdrop, 'so that my little brother Frost won't harm you.'

Snowdrop was sure she would not get even her arm into the little jacket, but she had hardly put a finger into the sleeve when the jacket started to stretch, to grow and grow, until it fitted her perfectly.

The old woman lifted her arms above her head and called out, 'Fly, fly my little children, my snow white stars, into the lap of your granny. I'll make a bouquet of you.'

Scarcely had she said these words, than it was as if the angels in the sky had torn up a feather bed. Snow flakes fell from the heavens. They danced and leaped, they circled and whirled

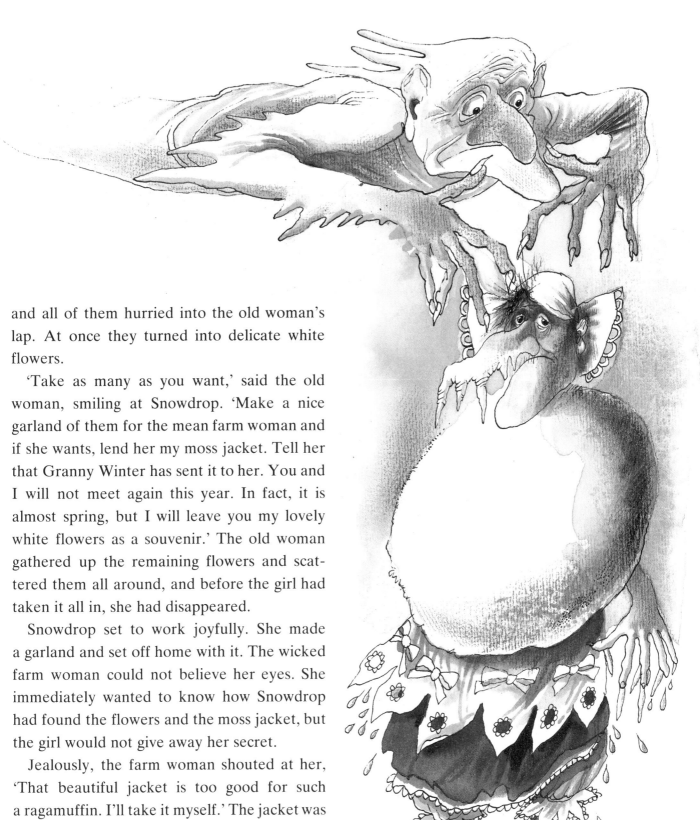

and all of them hurried into the old woman's lap. At once they turned into delicate white flowers.

'Take as many as you want,' said the old woman, smiling at Snowdrop. 'Make a nice garland of them for the mean farm woman and if she wants, lend her my moss jacket. Tell her that Granny Winter has sent it to her. You and I will not meet again this year. In fact, it is almost spring, but I will leave you my lovely white flowers as a souvenir.' The old woman gathered up the remaining flowers and scattered them all around, and before the girl had taken it all in, she had disappeared.

Snowdrop set to work joyfully. She made a garland and set off home with it. The wicked farm woman could not believe her eyes. She immediately wanted to know how Snowdrop had found the flowers and the moss jacket, but the girl would not give away her secret.

Jealously, the farm woman shouted at her, 'That beautiful jacket is too good for such a ragamuffin. I'll take it myself.' The jacket was tiny, just big enough for Snowdrop, but as soon as the woman had snatched it from the girl's shoulders, it started to grow and grow until it fitted the vain woman to perfection. She then plaited the garlands into her hair and looked with pleasure at her reflection in the mirror. It's a wonder she didn't die with shock! Looking back at her from the mirror was an ugly old hag. Her eyes were of ice, her nose was an icicle, her hair was hoar frost and the jacket had changed into a snowball. With that the door opened and an ice man with frozen claws pushed his way into the room. It was the North Wind.

'Come and dance with me, my bride!' he roared and caught the woman around her waist, dancing around the room with her.

Before Snowdrop could pull herself together they were gone and out of sight. Since then, the girl has managed the farm alone. She gets along very well. Only now and again, on long winter evenings, it seems to her that she can hear the sound of someone crying in the chimney.

People say that it is the wind wailing. Don't believe them. To this day, on cold winter evenings, you can hear the sound of the North Wind's bride crying in the chimney; and to this day also, in the meadow near the forest, where Snowdrop met the kind old lady, little white flowers bloom with each approaching spring. They cannot be harmed by frost or snow, for they are the grandchildren of Granny Winter. They have the same name as me. They are called snowdrops.

'Now I know, Snowdrop, why you are near to crying,' smiled the Rose Queen when she had heard the story. 'Because you have golden freckles on your nose from the spring sunshine.'

Snowdrop laughed and from her eye a single teardrop fell.

The Faithful Sunflower

She was a strange girl — the one with the golden rays around her fine head. She did not dance, she did not smile and she dismissed the joky young men with a cool nod of her head. She stood near the window all the time, gazing devotedly towards the sun. Only when twilight fell and the light round her hair dimmed did she bow her head thoughtfully and begin her story. This is how it went.

Before time began, impenetrable darkness ruled all the world. The Sun King was then living far, far away beyond the horizon and he never once stepped out of his glowing palace. Not a single one of his golden hairs escaped from there into the world to cut through never-ending darkness. High above only rain-bow fireworks twinkled, but it was not the sky and they were not stars. Arching over the wide, wide world was an endless blue meadow on which bloomed vast fields of magic flowers. In the flowers sat dainty nymphs singing sweet songs of love, while images of far away were reflected in their eyes. One day, the news of

their beauty reached the ears of the Sun King. The golden-haired ruler made a decision there and then.

'For the first time since the beginning of time I shall leave my palace to walk in the endless heavenly meadow. Among those magic flowers I want to find the most beautiful of the heavenly nymphs. She will become my wife,' he announced to his counsellors. The palace resounded with loyal cries of joy.

As it turned out, the handsome Sun King was very vain. He would stand all day in a room full of mirrors, beautifying his face with golden powder and ornamenting himself with sparkling jewels.

One day, he called a pretty young serving girl and gave her an order. 'Please take my most precious crystal mirror, climb up to the horizon and turn it towards the heavenly blue meadow,' he said. 'I want to see my royal charms from there, I want to enjoy my beauty.'

The little serving girl eagerly obeyed and as the Sun King walked regally through the heavenly meadow, she obligingly turned the crystal mirror this way and that so that all times he could see his face. It was while he was out walking that the golden hair of the Sun King shone with a blinding light, and darkness fled from the earth. The nymphs of heaven startled by this strange, unknown brilliance, fell from the sky on their magic flowers to the green earth below. The stars melted away. Only after the Sun King returned to his palace and darkness once more ruled over the world did they rise up quietly to the sky once more. But the seeds of their flowers let down their roots for all time into the fertile soil and that is how flowers came to the earth.

Since then, every morning, the Sun King sets out to look for his heavenly bride in the skies and every day his faithful serving girl follows him with the crystal mirror, but the moment the king steps out above the horizon, the stars always hide themselves in the soft embrace of the earth. He was never able to see them. One day the golden-haired ruler lost patience and burned with wild anger. Lightning flashed from his royal crown and his face in the crystal mirror was burning with a blinding light. The poor little serving girl was so scared, she dropped the mirror on to the earth where it broke into a thousand splinters.

'What have I done?' sobbed the girl and to avoid making the king any angrier, she took on the likeness of a handsome yellow flower in honour of the Sun King. Giving up his search for a bride, the king looked vainly towards the earth to see his reflection. What he saw, pleased him. He thought that he was looking into the crystal mirror at his own handsome likeness, and so in vain pride he set out towards the horizon to return to his golden palace. By now, he had given up hope of ever finding his chosen bride among the invisible heavenly nymphs, but enjoyed the quiet walks through the beautiful blue meadow.

From that time, day after day, he goes slowly from the east to the west and returns home again by way of secret underground paths – and day after day, I, the faithful Sunflower, turn my face towards the sun so that he may look upon his own handsome countenance.

Prince Midget

Still deep in thought from the Sunflower's story, the Rose Queen shed a dew tear. The tear changed into a little blue lake. On the blue lake floated a flock of white swans and in the lake's rainbow centre lay a splendid rose-coloured flower. A quiet, mysterious voice could be heard coming from the centre of the flower. 'I, the flower of the gods, am speaking to you,' it said. 'In the age-old legends of my homeland I am called the throne of the land. Today, I shall tell you a story about a country that is far away, set in the endless sea. Listen. It is I, the Lotus flower, who is speaking to you.' This is how the Lotus flower's story went.

On a certain mysterious island set in the sea there was a splendid Lotus kingdom. When the sun rose up out of the waves the powerful King of Light sat on the throne of the Lotus land, but as soon as the sun sank in the West and the first stars appeared in the sky, he handed his sceptre to his wife, the Queen of the Night Shadows. Both of them ruled wisely and justly. They loved each other, but even so, their hearts were heavy. They did not have a child to whom, someday, they could hand over rule of the lovely Lotus Island. The Queen of the Night Shadows therefore often cried on her moon throne and her teardrops fell unnoticed into the little lake at her feet.

One day, when the Queen of the Night Shadows was putting out the lights of the stars in the sky and the King of Light was just preparing to call up the sun from the waves, a little Lotus bud opened on the lake. In the chalice of the flower stood a little rose-coloured prince with moonlight hair who spoke humbly to the rulers.

'I am your son! A rose-coloured Lotus bud grew from the tears of my mother, and the sunbeams of my father caused the Lotus flower in which I was born to open.'

'Om nani padma hum,' said the King of Light. 'Look, there is a jewel in the Lotus flower,' and they were happy.

Nothing could spoil their joy. They were not even upset when they realized that the rosy prince remained the same size as he was when he first stepped from the Lotus flower. They began calling him Prince Midget. He was so tiny that at home he slept in a nutshell. The Queen of the Night Shadows bathed him in dew drops and allowed him to fly in the starlight on the wings of night moths. So the days passed.

One day Prince Midget called to his father in a tiny voice, 'My dear royal father, I've had enough of this boy life. I want to sail out to sea in my Lotus flower. I should like to see for myself where the sky sets its feet.'

'My foolish little one,' smiled the King of Light, 'if you were to sail right round the world, you would not find the feet of the sky. They will run away from you like your own shadow.'

The little prince's mind would not be changed, however. 'Do I not see with my own eyes how in the distance the sky meets the earth? Somewhere there the sky must have its feet. Otherwise, what would it stand on?' So he went on, begging and imploring his father for so long that the old king reluctantly gave way. He plucked the Lotus flower from the lake, set Prince Midget in it and carried it to the shore.

'My son, never part with the flower in which you were born,' he advised Prince Midget, 'for there is strength in it which will overcome evil and preserve life.'

The little prince pomised. Night came and the Queen of the Night Shadows lit the first stars in the sky.

'Goodbye, Mother,' Prince Midget called. Two teardrops fell into the Lotus flower and turned into rosy pearls. The prince sailed out to sea. He sailed for many days and for many nights, but the feet of the sky ran away from him all the time, and the horizon was always as far away as when he first set out. One day Prince Midget came to an unknown island. A fire was burning on the shore and around it danced huntsmen wearing plumes of bright feathers. On a tree nearby hung a bamboo cage. A wretched dog with a heavy stone tied to its neck and a scrawny cat on whose neck was tied a shrivelled coconut were imprisoned in the cage. The dog suddenly began to howl piteously. 'My brothers, large and small, you dogs who are serving people! I have sinned against the laws of my masters. I have stolen rice from the pots, I have eaten my masters' meat. For that, I have been punished. I must travel from village to village in this cage with the stone around my neck until I perish from hunger. My brothers, large or small, obey the laws of people or you will suffer the same fate.'

In the same way the scrawny cat gave vent to her anguish. 'My sisters, large or small, cats from the houses of people! I too have sinned against the laws of my masters. I stole baked fish from pans and licked cooked rice from the dishes. For that I have got into trouble. My sisters! Obey the laws of people, otherwise you will be destroyed by their anger!'

Prince Midget felt sorry for the wretched animals. 'Hey there, you brave hunters!' he called from his Lotus flower. 'What will you sell those unfortunate creatures for?'

'For two rosy pearls,' the hunters answered. The prince threw his pearls into the sand, the men floated the bamboo cage on the sea and tied it to the Lotus flower. Prince Midget once again set out on the endless sea, but the feet of the sky still escaped him.

One day the prince spoke to the animals. 'I will get rid of those ugly things that are weighing down your necks but you must promise me that you will not try to run away when we land on the coast.'

'I promise,' barked the dog. 'Dogs never betray those who have saved their lives. They would be breaking dogs' law, which matters more to them that the laws of people.'

'I promise too,' added the cat. 'Cats may only break promises given to mice. They are faithful to those they love. That is cats' law.'

The prince was pleased with their words and when at last they reached the shores of an unknown island, he released the animals from the cage.

'You are a wise prince,' said the dog, 'we are now more firmly tied to you than we were when we were in the flimsy bamboo cage. We are tied to you by gratitude.'

Prince Midget smiled, lifted the Lotus flower from the waves and pinned it in his hair. Then he set out with his friends to the centre of the island. It was a miserable journey. No flowers grew. There was not a single tree or bush and

the birds had flown away who knows where.

'We picked all the flowers as a mark of sorrow,' an old man they met on the way explained. 'The noble Princess Jasmine and all her friends were captured in the jungle by an evil witch. She was jealous of the beauty of our king's daughter. Jasmine flowers will no longer bloom in our country,' the old man lamented.

When the prince heard this he wasted no time. 'What's the point of looking for the feet of the sky when I can never find them,' he thought. 'I would rather release Princess Jasmine. It is time I looked for a bride anyway.'

He did as he said. Without delay, he and his faithful animals set out into the jungle to look for the evil witch. For a long time they wandered here and there until one day, they arrived at a hut made of butterfly wings. From out of the hut came a woman so beautiful that the prince held his breath. In place of hair she had a ball of black cobwebs and tiger eyes shone in her face.

'Oh noble ruler of the jungle,' said Prince Midget, bowing deeply. 'I have come for my bride, the Princess Jasmine.'

The witch laughed and said, 'Do you want to fight me for her, you little fool? You don't even come up to my ankles. Only if you drank a tear from my eye would you become as big and as powerful as I am, but you will never do that. Leave such vain talk and come inside where I'll refresh you with a drink of fresh flea blood, but first of all pull two cobweb hairs from my head and with them tie your horrible, ugly animals to a tree. They disgust me.'

The prince pretended to carry out her orders but instead, he used the hairs he had pulled out to tie the legs of the beautiful witch together. With an evil laugh the witch seized the little Prince and pushed him into her ear.

'What a fool you are! Now you will sing lullabies to your beautiful witch until the end of your life.'

At that moment, the Lotus flower called on a swarm of wild bees with her heady scent. The prince's faithful animals joined the swarm of bees in attacking the witch. The dog bit her leg, the cat sprang at her face and the bees stung her so much that she cried out and tears flowed from her eyes. She tried in vain to escape but her legs, tied together with her own hair, would not obey her. Prince Midget then jumped from her ear, held out his palm and drank a tear from her eye. Suddenly a strong and handsome young man stood before her and the witch turned into a small, ugly sprite. The prince

picked her up and imprisoned her in the petals of the Lotus flower.

'Where is Princess Jasmine?' he thundered at her.

'You will never get her, you accursed prince!' she hissed. 'There is a coconut palm growing in front of my hut which no living being is able to

climb. On top of the palm grows a coconut and inside that coconut sits your pretty princess, imprisoned till the end of time!'

Prince Midget did not know what to do and sat down on the ground in floods of tears, but the faithful cat began to climb up the palm tree.

Just when it seemed that the coconut was within reach of her paws, the crown of the tree started to grow higher and higher, until it was up above the clouds. As the cat's strength was failing, a brightly coloured bird circled the tree.

'If you will promise never again to hunt my

nestlings, I'll help you,' the bird called, 'but you must not break your promise, else terrible things will happen to Princess Jasmine.'

'I promise,' the cat replied, 'cats may break only promises made to mice. That is cats' law.'

With that, the brightly-coloured bird flew like a sparkling jewel up into the clouds, struck the coconut with its beak and let it drop at the feet of Prince Midget. As soon as the nut hit the ground, its shell burst open and from it poured out a troupe of courtiers adorned with pearls and gold. At the head of the procession was a lovely princess riding on a white tortoise and carrying a spray of jasmine.

'Oh, how beautiful she is,' the prince said, 'she is the most beautiful girl in all the world.' Straight away the Lotus flower opened and from its petals fell a cracked black pearl. It was the heart of the jealous witch. As if a magic wand had been waved, the island bloomed with sweet-smelling flowers and Prince Midget embraced his bride, Princess Jasmine.

So ends the story of how the little prince sought the feet of the sky and found happiness. He returned to his Lotus Kingdom and lived with his wife in peace and love. It was not long before he became the king, the most powerful ruler of a great kingdom in which the King of Light and the Queen of the Night Shadows are to this day lighting up the sun and the stars. Forever after, a rose-coloured Lotus flower blooms in the little lake and near the prince's throne sit his faithful animal friends, the dog and the cat.

The Little Milliner

'People call my brothers and sisters and me Everlasting Flowers,' said a little dancer in a straw hat, stepping forward. 'I will tell you how this came to be.'

In days long since passed, flowers could not boast of such lovely blooms as they can today. In those days, their heads were without hair, as shiny as chestnuts and as bald as those of human babies. They would cry with shame. Indeed, you all know how vain flowers are and how they want everyone to marvel at their beauty. One day they made up their minds to go out into the fields and meadows and to beg the fairies to give them some sort of hair. The fairies were happy to oblige. They made magic and chanted spells, they painted and varnished, here they did some cutting and there some curling. They gave one flower a rainbow colour rinse and another a sunshine tint. This one was shaded with evening mist and that one with the blush of the dawn sky. Afterwards, when the flowers looked at their reflections in the pool, their little hearts leapt for joy at all the beauty. However, there was one modest flower that had been over-looked. She waited patiently for her turn while the others pushed in front, elbowing each other out of the way. When at last it was her turn, the fairies did not feel like working any more, and all went off in different directions in search of other amusements.

The little flowers hid behind her happier sisters, crying and terribly ashamed of her poor, bare head. I will not tell you how the other flowers made fun of her. Flowers can be just as cruel as people. That day, the king himself was giving a gala ball in his golden palace. Princes, princesses, knights and musicians arrived from all corners of the world, all dressed in splendid attire. The flowers' new adornment went to their heads!

'Are we not beautiful enough to dance even with princes?' they egged each other on. One thing led to another and off went the flowers to the royal palace. Together they marched in a great procession trailing clouds of fragrance behind them, for the fairies had combed perfume into their hair, too! At the back of the procession trotted the unhappy little flower, hoping that she would at least be able to look into the palace through the keyhole. Of course she herself would not dare to go to the royal ball with her own bare little head.

At that time, there was a little milliner living near the foot of the castle. Her parents had died long ago and she was living alone, poor as a church mouse. To add to her woes, she had fallen ill and had not even the strength to go to the well for water.

'Good people, do please fetch me a jug of water and I will show my gratitude by giving you a hat, whichever one you choose,' she called to passers-by from her window. On such a special day no one seemed to notice the poor girl's misfortune. Everybody was rushing to the palace so as not to miss the glorious sights. When the procession of flowers streamed past, the little milliner called to them, but they just chattered away to each other, ignoring the young girl's pleas for help.

'We have no time, we are hurrying to the royal ball,' they called to her. 'What good would your hats be to us, anyway? Don't you see what beautiful hair we have?'

Only the unhappy little flower took pity on the poor milliner. She took the jug, drew water from the well and brought it right into the milliner's home. The poor thing felt better at once! The sad little flower cleaned the milliner's house, put the poor little thing to bed, warmed the covers with her breath and blew soothingly on her fevered brow.

'You are as sad as I am,' said the little milliner looking searchingly at the flower. 'What has happened to upset you?'

The little flower told the milliner what had happened and how much she would like to see the royal ball, even if it were only through the keyhole. 'How can I even think of doing such a thing?' she wailed. 'Just look at my poor head. Everyone there would make fun of me.'

The milliner laughed. 'That is easily put right,' she said. 'Put this little straw hat on your head. It will suit you.'

So the everlasting flower did as she said, thanked her and feeling very happy, set off after her sisters to the royal palace. How splendid it was! Everything was glittering like stars. All those noble guests! Those princes, knights and haughty ladies. The loveliest of them all, however, were the flowers. Their partners would not let them leave the dance floor, or even stop for breath! The modest little flower stood in a corner and marvelled at all the splendour.

When the handsome Spring Prince entered the ballroom in a cloak of May showers all the flowers bloomed with such grace and fragrance that their partners grew dizzy with it all. Then when the noble Summer Prince in his golden

robes and crown of sun rays was announced, they became quite intoxicated with his charm. The young men of the court knelt at their feet and begged at least to be permitted to breathe their perfume. Then, when the ball was at its height, the Autumn King made his entrance. He was shrouded in black clouds from which a cold wind blew. Nestled in his tangled hair was a crown of dried leaves and muddy rainwater gushed from his eyes. The vain flowers huddled shivering in the arms of their partners and their splendid curly hair began to wither and fall, until their heads were quite bare again. In shame, the flowers rushed out into the gardens, meadows, forests and fields. They hid themselves there and waited through the whole long winter until the Spring Prince returned with his host of magic fairies.

Only the modest little flower in her everlasting straw hat remained. She looked so sweet that a handsome young prince fell in love with her then and there and asked her to marry him.

They had many children and those children in turn had children. All those flower children went to the little milliner for hats, and each hat she made for them was different, but each as lovely as the other.

Since then, everlasting flowers have not withered or fallen, even when people picked them. In winter, as in summer, they live on unchanged.

The Miller's Daughters

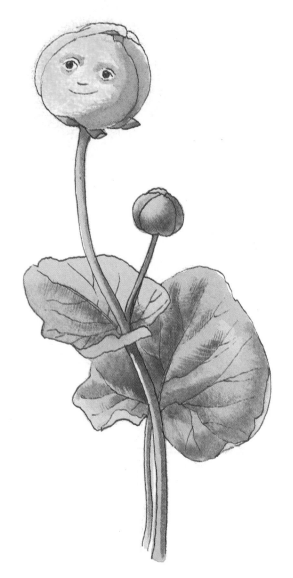

'There was once a miller who was a widower. He had a very lovely daughter. She was very kind and everybody loved her,' the shapely Marsh Marigold began, smiling at the Rose Queen. 'I wonder if I can remember the name of that girl?' she pondered. 'Yes, I know! they called her Flora. That was her name.'

One day, Flora turned to her father, the old miller, and stroked his grey hair. 'Daddy,' she said, 'you treat me as the apple of your eye. You fulfil my every wish before I can even speak it. I am very happy here with you, but not truly content in my heart. I should like to have someone to share my girlish secrets. Please find me a new mother.'

The miller tried to change the girl's mind, but when she could not be dissuaded, he started looking around for a wife. His eye was taken by a good-looking young widow who had a daughter about the same age as Flora. She was all fun and laughter and had a honeyed tongue while her daughter behaved to Flora as if she were really her sister. The widow gladly accepted the miller's offer of marriage and it was not long before their wedding was celebrated at the mill.

There's no denying that up to the wedding, both the widower and Flora were fine! The bride-to-be would have brought them the moon and her daughter behaved in the same way, but the moment she became the miller's wife, the mill truly became a place of misery. Wherever she went, Flora's stepmother complained. She left no one in peace, and her sharp tongue lashed out frequently at the miller and Flora.

feel sorry for asking her father to take a bride, but she did not dare to complain to him. Indeed, he was suffering as well and when, now and again, he stood up for his daughter, those two bullies almost tore him to shreds.

Flora felt she could no longer stand this suffering, so one day she tied a few things in a bundle and crept out of the mill. 'I'll go out into the world and seek service,' she decided.

The stepmother and her daughter, who was called Teresa, were like two peas in a pod. Teresa hardly ever answered when she was spoken to, she was lazy as could be and her peevish moods and lies were beyond counting. Flora had certainly fallen on hard times. Her stepmother did not allow her to rest a moment, she scolded her for every little thing, while she spoiled her own daughter, petting and indulging her. Flora had to do the most unpleasant jobs at the mill and, as well, she had to serve Teresa. At meal time she was given dry crusts and was only allowed to sleep in the porch. It was too late to

She walked and walked until she came to a large marshy meadow full of marsh marigolds in bloom. There was a merry little brook gurgling in the middle of the meadow with a narrow foot-bridge over it. 'God be with you, little foot-bridge,' Flora greeted it. 'Please let me pass over to the other bank and I'll think well of you.'

'Of course I'll let you, why shouldn't I?' replied the foot-bridge. 'Just be so good as to turn me over. My back is aching from all those pounding feet that pass over me.'

The girl did as the footbridge had asked and the foot-bridge then asked her where she was going. 'Out into the world to look for service, dear little bridge,' Flora confided, 'only I've no idea where I should look.'

'Take the loveliest marsh marigold from my meadow. It will bring you good luck,' the foot-bridge advised her and they parted in a friendly way. After a while, Flora arrived at a place where three roads met. One path was made of copper, one of silver and the third of gold.

'Which way should I take?' The girl wondered. At that, a little golden fairy peeped out of the marsh marigold. 'Gold means bad luck,

silver does not foretell anything good. The girl with the yellow flower should take the copper path,' the fairy advised her and immediately hid once more inside the flower.

Flora thanked her nicely and set out along the copper path. As she went, the path behind her disappeared, leaving no trace. In no time Flora reached an impassable blackberry thicket. 'God be with you, dear blackberries,' the girl greeted them. 'Be so good as to let me continue along my path!'

Although it was spring, the branches were bending beneath the weight of ripe blackberries. The thicket answered, 'Do you not see how weary I am under the weight of my fruit? If you lighten my burden by picking some blackberries to take with you, I shall let you pass with the grace of God.'

The girl hurried to pick the sweet fruit and the thicket opened up before her like a garden gate. In time, Flora reached a dogrose thicket. The copper path wound among the thorns and still the end was not in sight. The bushes were red with ripe hips and when the girl promised the dogroses that she would gladly pick some of the fruit to lessen the weight, the thicket of itself opened up before her so that she did not touch a single thorn.

Finally, the copper path took Flora to a high cliff. There were three figure doors engraved on the cliff. One was made of copper, the second of silver and the third of gold. Flora did not know what to do.

The little fairy then peeped out of the marsh marigold and said, 'Gold means misfortune, silver does not foretell anything good. Obey the marsh marigold fairy and knock on the copper door!'

Flora did as she said and banged on the copper door, which opened wide before her.

The astonished girl stood in a large cave. There was a huge spider's web hanging from the ceiling of the cave and in it sat an ugly old woman, combing her hair with a red-hot copper comb.

'God be with you, granny,' Flora said boldly. 'I have been guided to you by the copper path. Please take me into your service.' The old woman cackled, saying, 'And why not take two sacks and climb into the oven. There you will find three little caves. In one there is darkness like at midnight, in the second light as at midday. I want you to clean out the two caves, and mind you do a proper job. You will tie up both the darkness and the light nicely into the sacks. I warn you, however, do not even glance into the third cave or something terrible will happen to you.'

With that, the old hag sat astride a red-hot broomstick and flew off somewhere for a gossip.

The poor girl had no idea what to do. Flames leaped from the oven as from the jaws of a dragon. So she begged the marsh marigold fairy to help her. 'There is nothing to be afraid of,' the fairy said comfortingly. 'I'll go in front of you and make a path for you through the fire,' and she did as she promised. Flora crawled after her into the flames which miraculously parted in front of the marsh marigold fairy so that not one of them burned her. In this way, they safely reached the first little cave. This cave was so dark you could not see one step ahead, the fairy lost no time, and opening the flower of the marsh marigold, she used it to scoop up the pitch-black darkness and pour it into the sack. In a minute the cave was lit up as if filled with sunshine. There was no trace of the darkness. The fairy then poured the light from the other cave into the second sack and all of a sudden it grew as dark as midnight.

'We have succeeded,' the marsh marigold fairy said, with a smile. 'From now on you must manage by yourself,' she said, and disappeared without a trace.

'However shall I get out of the fiery oven?' Flora thought to herself, but soon her curiosity got the better of her fear. 'What could there be in the third cave?' she wondered, and taking her courage in both hands, peeped in with one eye. Wonder of wonders, in the middle of the grotto sparkled a clear little lake with brightly coloured water lilies floating on its surface. Flora's head span with the splendour of it all. She could not resist stepping into the cool water to refresh herself. As she swam, one blossom after another became tangled in her hair and when at last she climbed back on to the bank, her head was a cluster of blooms. The flowers were of gold and silver and as she shook the water from her hair, pearls fell at her feet. Flora decided it would be best not to stay any longer and picking up her sacks, hurried out of the oven. The flames parted before her as though she was waving a magic wand and almost before she knew it, she stood once again in the large cave – face to face with the angry old hag.

'Just you wait, you are going to be sorry for this!' hissed the witch, making a swipe at Flora's hair with her red-hot comb to comb the flowers out. With ease, the girl slipped like a snake from her grasp and ran away from the cave as fast as her legs would carry her, forgetting that she still had the old hag's sacks with her.

Outside, it was so dark that the poor girl could not see a step in front of her. She fell into holes, bumped against trees and had no idea which way to go. On top of it all, she was so weighed down by the sacks that she was out of breath, so she untied the sacks of light and poured it out before her along the way. At once it grew light and Flora saw the dogrose thicket not far in front. She clasped her hands, asked nicely, and a narrow little path opened up through the thorny thicket, closing again as soon as she passed – and just in time for the old hag was hot on her heels and almost touching

her hair with the red-hot comb. Before the old crone could free herself from the thorns, Flora was far ahead. Not for long, though, for in no time the evil witch was at her heels again.

Quite out of breath, Flora reached the blackberry thicket. She greeted the thicket, asked nicely and the blackberry branches let her through. Once more the witch became entangled. She was not about to give up that easily however, and she put on her magic clogs. These clogs took her seven miles with every step, and before long she was once more reaching out her claws towards poor Flora. In despair, the girl untied the second sack and tipped out the darkness behind her. Before the old crone could light her way with her fiery eyes, Flora heard the gurgling of the brook in the nearby meadow.

'Little foot-bridge, please save me,' she begged and the grateful foot-bridge readily carried her over to the other bank. The old hag came rushing up like a hurricane, panting and curs-

ing, reaching out to Flora's hair with her red-hot comb. The moment she stepped on to the footbridge however, it gave way beneath her and the good little brook carried her far, far away, maybe even as far as the sea. Poor Flora nearly collapsing from exhaustion hardly knew how she reached the mill and her home.

Her father cried for joy that his daughter had come back, but the evil stepmother and her stepsister were ready to burst with envy. They immediately asked Flora how she came by the precious flowers in her hair. Before the kind girl had finished telling them, they were dressing for a journey, nothing could hold them back. The journey took them a long time. When they arrived at the brook, they did not greet the little foot-bridge and so it did not allow them to cross. The two evil women had to go upstream till they found the ford.

They did at last come to the place where the roads met, though. Here, one path was silver, the other golden. They each took one. Through the blackberry thicket, through the dogrose thicket, their strength exhausted, they finally reached the high cliff. They knocked at the silver door and the golden door and when the doors opened, they rushed impatiently in. The doors closed noisily behind them and those envious women have not been seen since.

'Gold means misfortune and silver foretells nothing good,' said the delicate marsh marigold ending her tale with a smile as radiant as the full moon itself.

'What about Flora with the gold and silver flowers in her hair?' asked the Rose Queen.

'Oh, the king soon heard of her bravery. It impressed him so much he asked her to be his bride,' replied the marsh marigold.

Lazybones and his Spider Bride

'Long, long ago, in a far-off land, there was a most peculiar kingdom,' a plump little princess in a billowing white dress began. This little princess looked very much like a snowball. In fact, she looked so much like a snowball that that was what everyone called her. This is how Snowball's story went on.

All the people living in that kingdom were shoemakers and cobblers. No one knew how to do anything but to use the awl, to repair heels, to cut out tops of boots from leather and to spank cobbler's children with the cobbler's stirrup. Why, even the king used to sit on a shoemaker's stool instead of a throne. The people of the kingdom had been cobblers for so long they couldn't remember when it had all begun and what was the name of the first cobbler in the land. It was not surprising, therefore, that no one could find any other kind of work. Everyone had more shoes than they would ever need, but they all lived from hand to mouth. Nobody wanted to work in the fields or even try their hand at another trade.

Now, in this strange kingdom there lived a young cobbler called Lazybones. Day and night he lounged around at home in the warm and it never even occurred to him to go outside the house.

'You ought to go out into the world and learn another trade or the whole family will soon die of hunger,' said his father, who was also a cobbler, of course.

The young man answered with a laugh, 'You are a cobbler, I am a cobbler, grandfather and great-grandfather were also cobblers. It would be a sorry state of affairs if I should be the one to break the family tradition.'

'One day the young man's mother decided enough was enough. She spoke to him sharply, saying he should at least get married.

'Oh yes, Mother, I'll get married,' Lazybones laughed. 'But it will be when this stove I am resting my feet on goes out into the world of its own accord. Then I shall marry the first woman who does not refuse me.'

Hardly had he uttered these words than, strange to tell, the stove rolled with him out of the door and straight to the inn where a dance was in progress. Lazybones was astonished, but what could he do? A promise is a promise. He turned on his stove to the prettiest dancer and at once asked her for a dance – and what a dance

it was! The music played and the stove danced with the startled girl, twisting and twirling and skipping about till it rattled and clanked and up there on top, Lazybones laughed till his poor sides ached.

'Would you like to marry me?' he asked the worn-out woman as the band played a tune in their honour.

'What can you do?' she asked.

'I know how to mend shoes,' the cobbler's apprentice declared with pride, but the girl just pulled a face and shook her head. Cobblers were easy to find in that kingdom. So like it or not, Lazybones had to go out into the world on his stove. Wherever he went he asked all the girls he came across if they would marry him, but no one would have him. It was no wonder. Who would want a cobbler in the shoemakers' kingdom?

Then one evening, Lazybones reached a dark forest. The dark was so deep you could almost cut it with a knife. The wind moaned and sighed in the trees, and Lazybones could feel prickles running up and down his spine. All of a sudden, a gang of robbers jumped out in front of Lazybones. Every one of the robbers was as big as a mountain, with long black hair and a thick black beard and eyes like glowing embers. Their commander had a gold ring in his nose and behind him stood his daughter, wild and lovely as a doe from the forest. They were all aiming their guns at Lazybones.

'Your money, or your life!' the robber chief roared at the poor fellow. Lazybones's blood froze in his veins and the stove was also trembling with fear. Suddenly there came a rumbling from its innards. Huge clouds of smoke and enormous flames shot out of its grate and the stove started rolling straight at those greedy robbers.

'Save yourselves, it's a dragon!' they shouted, stumbling over each other as they ran away in all directions. Only the robber's daughter had not managed to get away. Lazybones caught her by her plait and at once begged her to tell him whether she would like to marry him.

'I have an honest trade, I know how to mend shoes,' he told her proudly, but the beautiful wild creature was horrified.

'You say you want to marry me, yet why do you want to punish me?' she cried. 'My great-grandfather was a robber, my grand-father was a robber, my father and mother are robbers and you expect me to start living honestly? It would make my ancestors turn in their graves,' and before Lazybones knew what she was about, she took out her knife, cut off her plait and was gone.

'Drat the cobbler's trade!' the young man grumbled and set out again on his stove. He travelled all night and half the next day. When the sun was high in the sky, the cobbler started to feel unpleasantly hot on the stove. He could hardly breathe it was so hot and his mouth was parched with thirst. Just then, he saw an old woman on the roadside. She was wearing three sheepskin coats and on her head were three sheepskin caps. Around her neck she wore three woollen scarves. There she sat, shivering with cold, poor thing. Lazybones felt sorry for her. 'Come on, granny, on to my stove,' he said.

'It is so hot here that you could fry pancakes on your hand. That should warm you up.'

'On top of the stove? What must you be thinking of, dear fellow! At the very least I would have to climb into the oven or I'll die of cold,' said the old lady and before Lazybones could say another word, there she was, sitting in the oven.

'Oh, that's lovely and warm!' said the old woman, flames licking her face. Seeing her pleasure, Lazybones got down from the stove with a smile and put another bundle of wood on the fire.

'I like you, old lady. Besides that, you're fire proof! Wouldn't you like to marry me?' he asked politely. Deep in his heart, however, he was trembling with worry in case the old woman said yes. What could he do with such an old, worn-out creature!

'What can you be thinking of, young fellow?' the old lady laughed. 'I am 300 years old and getting married is far from my thoughts, but because you have been so good to me, I'll give you some advice. Not far from here you will find a snowball bush. Use the magic words and your wish will be answered.'

So saying, the old lady whispered the magic words into Lazybones's ear. After speaking, she vanished in a puff of smoke. The young cobbler wasted no time and set off in the direction of the snowball bush. Before long he reached a stone castle. This castle was not like an ordinary castle; it was tiny like a doll's castle. Inside this castle bloomed a snowball bush.

Lazybones then spoke the magic words told to him by the old woman. 'All flowers are beautiful but loveliest of all is the snowball. Please, be my guide and show me my bride.'

With that, the snowball bush shook as though a breeze were blowing through its branches. It lifted itself up to the sun and stretched out its most beautiful flower towards Lazybones.

'Here I am, here I am,' a tiny little voice called.

Lazybones looked and looked, but could see nothing except a little spider weaving its silver cobweb like a wedding veil around the flower.

'Saints preserve us!' cried Lazybones, throwing up his hands in horror. 'Am I expected to marry a spider bride?' No help came, however, and a promise is a promise especially a cobbler's promise which sticks like cobbler's glue.

Hoping the spider wouldn't hear, Lazybones

whispered as softly as he could, 'Would you care to marry me, spider girl?'

'I should be glad to,' the little spider replied and that was that!

What could poor Lazybones do? He set his little bride nicely on his hat and went off into the world to look for some proper work. It wasn't as if the lazy chap was eager to find a job, but his spider bride insisted. Before long they reached a foreign kingdom. No matter where you looked, the only work anyone seemed to know how to do was tailoring. Even the king himself was seated on a tailor's stool, diligently plying his needle and thimble. No one there knew how

to make shoes however. They all went about barefooted.

'There will be no shortage of work here,' said the little spider, 'but before anything else, you must build us a house.' Lazybones didn't very much like the idea of this, but when his bride insisted, he set to and before long a little house, neat as a pin, stood before them. Out of habit, Lazybones at once hopped on to the stove.

'Enough of that!' the little spider said crossly. 'Off with you, you idle fellow, and find some work.'

Not wasting another moment, the little spider went all over the house, cleaning as she went, until it was so clean it sparkled.

Lazybones did not want to be outshone by a spider. Anyway, in that barefooted kingdom he soon had more work than he could cope with and money poured in from all sides. In the end, the shoemaker became quite fond of his work, but there was one thing that he could not understand. Every night when he went to bed, a beautiful but sad princess appeared in his room.

'Take me for your wife,' she pleaded, crying.

Lazybones could not keep his eyes away from her and every night he almost found himself falling in love with her but always remembered in time his own loving and industrious spider bride.

'Do please forgive me, Miss Princess, but I am promised for the rest of my life,' he told the beautiful young woman. 'Find someone in the world who is your equal. Whatever would you do with a cobbler like me?'

Each time the princess would cast him a pleading glance and then disappear. When the time came that all people in the kingdom had shoes for special occasions and shoes for work, the little spider decided it was time to pay a visit

song took them back to the little stone castle where the snowball bush grew.

'Do you remember? This is where we met,' the little spider called. 'Let's just stop in here and think for a while.' The cobbler had no objections to this for the nearer they came to his home, the more he wanted to dawdle. He was afraid he and his spider bride would be made fun of, so he climbed down from the stove and sat on the ramparts of the little castle, with his little spider in the palm of his hand.

Suddenly the castle shook and began to grow. It grew and grew until it had grown into a splendid palace with roofs of gold. Before he had realized what happened, Lazybones found himself high up in the clouds on the top of a turret. In his arms was the very princess that had appeared to him at night.

'Thank you, my dear husband. You have freed me from a magic spell. You remained faithful to me during the most difficult times,' said the lovely princess and from her pocket she took a cobweb handkerchief. They both stood on this and together they floated down to the castle courtyard. As far as the eye could see, lovely snowball flowers were blooming. As Lazybones looked, knights, armour bearers, footmen, cooks and serving maids appeared from the flowers and all joyously ran to greet the princess and her bridegroom.

'You will no longer be a shoemaker, but the king of Snowball Kingdom,' the princess smiled, and gave orders for the cobbler's parents to be brought to the castle. Then a great wedding took place, the like of which had never been seen before. Lazybones took it into his head to make two little pairs of dancing shoes – one for himself and one for the princess.

When he had finished, the celebrations began and they danced and danced until morning.

to Lazybones's parents. The shoemaker was not very keen, for he was afraid that all the apprentices at home would make fun of him, but the stove started to smoke and burn and set out on the journey of its own accord. Lazybones only just managed to swing himself up on to it. He looked around for his bride and then he noticed that a white cockerel was flying in front of the stove with the little spider seated on its back.

'Cock-a-doodle-doo! Out of the spider princess's way! She's taking the cobbler to her palace without delay,' sang the cockerel and Lazybones laughed. Before long this merry

Everyone was happy except for the bride, who was shedding tears as big as peas. 'Why ever is my bride crying?' said Lazybones.

His father then took him aside. 'You're a fine shoemaker!' he scolded. 'Don't you see that the shoes made for your bride to dance in are too small? Thank goodness you have left the trade. Rather work at being a king.'

Hearing these words Lazybones ran to help his poor bride take her little shoes off.

Beautiful Marguerite

The Rose Queen's eye was taken by a good-looking girl in a bright hat. The hat was yellow with a rim of pure white petals. The girl was tearing off these petals, one after the other, and saying quietly, 'He loves me, he loves me not. He loves me, he loves me not.'

'What a pity to spoil that lovely hat, dear Daisy,' the Rose Queen called to her. 'Tell us a story instead.' This is the story the daisy told.

A long time ago in a far-off village lived a young girl called Marguerite. She was seven times lovelier than all the young girls far and near, but she was seven times poorer than the poorest beggar. She had no family in the whole wide world. So as not to die of hunger, she took up service in the mill. This mill belonged to a very ugly miller. His nose hung down between his knees, he had bat ears and huge fiery eyes. In fact, he was not a man but a wizard. No one ever saw farmers carrying grain to the mill, no one went anywhere near it, but even so, the mill turned and turned and instead of flour, magic gold pieces fell into the sacks. When Marguerite arrived there, she was very frightened, but soon pulled her wits together.

'Good day, Mr Miller,' she greeted him. 'I am coming here as a servant girl. I am not afraid of work and I'll obey your every word if only you will give me something to eat.'

The miller looked at her fiercely, gave a loud rasping laugh and said gruffly, 'Well, well, my delicate beauty! You have enough courage to stop the mill wheels turning. We'll see how you get on at work.' As he spoke mice jumped out of his ghoulish mouth.

At this sight, Marguerite was almost ready to change her mind about staying but the miller seemed to read her thoughts. 'During the day, you'll never get away from me easily, I'll guard you well, but at night — let's wait and see,' the evil wizard laughed. He ordered her to take a sickle and go to the meadow to fetch grass for his little horse. With a stout heart Marguerite took up a basket and ran to the meadow. She wielded her sickle and cut and cut. In a short while the basket was overflowing. Marguerite tried to lift it on to her back, but the basket seemed to be nailed down. Looking into it, Marguerite saw that instead of green grass, the old wicker basket contained blades of pure gold. A giant wouldn't be able to lift that

weight. At a loss as to what to do next, the girl sat down on the basket. In a trice the basket rose up by itself and flew straight into the miller's stable where a strange looking horse stood. He had one head at the front and another at the back and two tails near each head. His legs ended in cow's hooves. With great gusto, it started on the gold grass. The miller was very pleased.

'You have done well, Marguerite. I can see that you know how to put your hand to work. I shan't need you any more today.'

The girl wandered back to the meadow, sat down in the grass and began to weave a beautiful daisy into her hair. She remembered that her mother had told her that daisies help to ward off evil magic and spells.

As twilight fell, the miller called Marguerite, took his horse out of the stable and said, 'Tonight I am going off to the executioner's yard to dance with the hanged men, but I'll deal with you before I go. I know very well what is in your head. The moment my back is turned, you will be looking around for a way to escape.'

Before Marguerite knew what had happened, she had turned into a little picture. The miller hung the picture on the wall, cracked his magic whip and off he went on his strange horse.

That evening, a young man arrived at the mill. He was on his travels and so as not to be lonely on his way, he carried a black tomcat in his satchel. Hungry and thirsty, his feet hardly able to carry him, he was glad at last to find a roof over his head.

'Mr Miller, Mr Miller,' he called, but no answer came. The only sound was that of the mill wheel merrily clacking and instead of flour, gold coins poured into the sacks. 'That's a strange state of affairs,' said the young man, scratching his head. He began to look around.

There on the wall he saw the picture of Marguerite. She was so lovely he fell in love with her straight away.

'That's the girl I want for my wife and no other,' the young man sighed. As he spoke, the daisy fell from the girl's hair. The young man stepped back in surprise. He picked up the flower and began picking off its petals, one by one.

'She loves me, she loves me not. She loves me, she loves me not. She loves me!' he cried joyfully as he plucked the last petal. At that moment, all the petals grew on the daisy once more and out of the picture sprang Marguerite and fell into the young man's arms. She fell in love with him then and there, and told him

everything; all about how lonely she was and how the evil wizard had trapped her in the picture so she could not escape. They took each other by the hand and ran down the path as though their heels were on fire. They ran and ran until they were out of breath and their feet could hardly carry them, but they were right back where they had started from! There were many paths that seemed to lead away from the mill but no matter how far they ran they got nowhere. Marguerite began to cry but then they heard the thundering of hooves coming nearer and nearer. Quickly she jumped back into the picture, only to find she had left the daisy in the young man's hand. The evil wizard had come back!

'What are you doing here?' he roared.

'Why, I am nothing but an honest workman, looking for work, your honour,' the young man replied. The miller's laugh was as musical as a herd of elephant's stampeding through a gravel patch.

'Good. I'll give you a job,' he declared. 'If you can catch every word that falls from my mouth, you may take from my mill whatever you want and go about your own business again – but woe betide you if you fail!'

All at once the miller began to mutter magic words through his devilish lips as fast as he could. As each word fell from his mouth it turned at once into a mouse and soon mice were squeaking and chasing all around the mill as though they were at a ball. The young man lost no time. He opened his satchel and let out his black cat. Before you could say Jack Robinson, all the mice were lying dead at the young man's feet. Not one was missing. The miller scowled.

'All right. You have won,' he said. 'Take a sack of gold pieces and be off to where you come from.' The young man shook his head.

'You're wrong there, Mr Miller, that's not what we agreed,' he said. 'I'll take the thing I like most here. This little picture.'

At once the beautiful Marguerite jumped out of the picture and ran to the young man's arms. The miller frowned.

'Well, if that's what you want!' he said, curtly, 'but before she goes, Marguerite must cut grass for my little horse once more.' The young man agreed to this. He helped Marguerite with the basket and they went to the meadow together. There they found as many young reaper girls as seeds in a poppy head, each one more beautiful than the next; Marguerite, however, was seven times more beautiful than the most beautiful of them. Straight away she began to swing her sickle. At that moment, the ugly miller was standing there. Three times he turned on his heel, three times he clapped his hands and three times flames shot from his mouth. The young man's head span from the shock of it all. There before him, instead of lovely reaper girls, spread a carpet of beautiful flowers. They filled the meadow from end to end each one lovely, and each one different from the one before. Which of them was Marguerite? The young man was lost in despair.

'If you can't find your bride among the flowers by evening, she will be changed for ever into a black spider,' the miller roared and so saying, he disappeared.

The young man was at his wits' end, and his black tomcat could not help him, either. He sat sorrowfully in the grass and poured out his grief to all the lovely flowers. Just then a white daisy tapped his hat. It was the very one which had been placed there by his beloved Marguerite. The young man clapped his hands with joy.

'I've got it! Why didn't I think of it before?' he cried, and, taking the little daisy in his hand, set out from flower to flower. 'She loves me, she loves me not. She loves me, she loves me not,' he recited as he knelt before every flower and plucked the white petals from the daisy. Each time it came out 'she loves me not', and each time, the petals once more grew on the daisy.

It was now late afternoon and the sun was beginning to sink in the west. The young man was in despair. He could not find Marguerite anywhere. When only the rim of the sun showed above the horizon, the young man arrived at a modest, fragile little flower. She was simple and small and she looked like a younger sister of his daisy. The young man once more plucked the petals of the daisy, reciting the words as before. 'She loves me, she loves me not. She loves me!' he cried in delight. The simple little flower at once changed back into Marguerite. She was now seven times more beautiful than she was before. She hugged her young man and all the flowers on the meadow turned away shyly. At that moment, the two-headed, four-tailed horse galloped out of the stable with the ugly miller on his back. Three times they circled the mill, three times the horse struck its hooves against the ground and then the earth opened up and swallowed them, leaving behind them only the sacks full of gold coins.

As for Marguerite and her young man, they are living to this day in the mill where they no longer grind out gold coins but grain as a proper mill should. In that meadow, where Marguerite used to cut the golden grass, fragile white flowers now bloom every spring. They are as sweet and lovely as charming little Marguerite and in fact, that is what people call them.

Thirty

'I'm at home anywhere,' said Princess Mullein, in her fluffy coat and with yellow flowers in her hair. 'I don't need much to make me happy — a handful of poor soil and perhaps a little bedtime story. If you like, I'll tell you one from France. Listen!'

There was once a little hill, and on that hill a little house, and in that little house a little table. At that little table a lazy young man used to sit all day long. There was no denying the boy was well-built, handsome and had strength enough for thirty like him. In fact, that is what they called him. His name was Thirty. Strong he may have been, this fellow, Thirty, but he was so lazy, words cannot describe it. Neighbours would shake their heads over it and often asked his mother where her son got such strength.

'How do I know?' his mother would reply. 'Perhaps it is because I used to make him tea from the flowers of the mullein. What good is his strength to me though, when he doesn't lift a finger to do anything the whole day long. Sometimes it seems to me that he is so lazy, the stool he sits on has grown to the seat of his trousers.'

Thirty's mother grumbled and grumbled like this, until one day the young man was tired of it. 'Hold your tongue, mother! If nothing else will

please you, then I'll go down into the valley and offer myself for work as a farmhand!'

This, however, was easier said than done! Thirty wasn't used to taking a single step without a specific purpose and now he wasn't sure exactly how to make such a journey. So he tumbled off the stool in a grumpy mood and rolled headlong down the hill right into the valley. On the way he dislodged a great pile of stones. The farmer was building some new cowsheds and the stones came in very handy.

'Say, friend, I could do with a good worker such as yourself,' he said. 'How would you like to stay on here as a farmhand?'

'That's why I've come,' Thirty answered. 'First though, don't you think you should pay me for that work with the stones?'

The farmer agreed, and said Thirty could take home as much wheat as he could carry on his back. The farmer did not know Thirty, however, and had no idea that Thirty would be able to carry all the sacks from the granary floor in one go.

When Thirty rolled up for work the next day,

his master ordered him to go to the forest to bring back firewood. Before you could say Jack Robinson, Thirty was back again carrying the whole forest in a bundle on his back.

'Who wants to make two trips for firewood?' he laughed. 'In case you don't know, I am a very lazy chap. That's what my mother claims. Now, I must admit, I'm very hungry.'

His master was afraid that such a great hulk of a fellow would eat him out of house and home in one go, so he began to get nervous. 'Well, my lad, you can't get water out of a stone. There was a big drought and the crops failed. You'll have to climb a tree in the orchard and get yourself some fruit.'

Well, that idea didn't appeal to Thirty at all. Who could imagine him climbing trees? So, instead, he seized the bridle of his master's best horse and hurled him into the crown of the tree until pears fell down like a hailstorm. Of course, the horse was killed, and the farmer, frightened out of his wits, racked his brains to find a clever way of getting rid of this giant. He hesitated about throwing him out in case the young giant started a fight. Then the farmer had what he thought was a good idea.

'Listen, young man! You are a strong fellow such as I have never seen the like, and that's for sure, but I'll bet you couldn't bring the Devil on your back from Hell.'

'Why not?' demanded Thirty.

'Could you ask him for a sack of gold as well?'

'Of course!' growled the young man.

So they shook hands on it, the wager being the sack of gold from Hell. The farmer rubbed his hands together, thinking what a clever fellow he was.

Meanwhile, Thirty looked around for some sort of weapon. He noticed a pair of coal tongs on the ground. 'Look out, Devil. I'm coming to get you,' he cried. 'If only it were not so far to Hell!' he moaned, and because he was such a lazy fellow, he tossed an oak bedstead over his

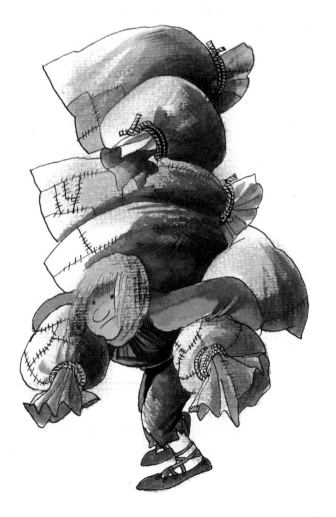

shoulder so that he had somewhere to rest on the way.

The journey took a long time. That's hardly surprising considering how much time Thirty had spent snuggled up in bed. Finally, though, he arrived at the gates of Hell. He banged on the gate until Hell shook.

'Who's that?' the Devil himself called out.

'It's me,' the young man replied.

'Who is me?' the Devil wondered.

'Thirty,' the strong man thundered. 'Open at once or your gate will soon look like a colander.' The Devil was startled. He thought there were thirty such hooligans outside the gate and rushed to open it, not knowing what he had let

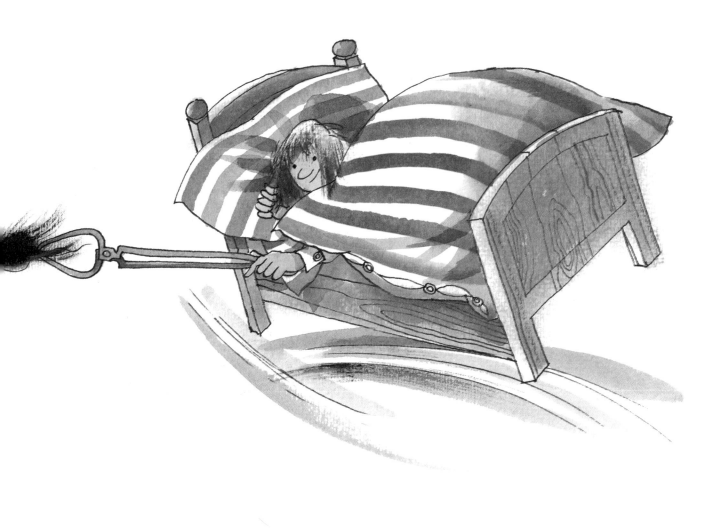

himself in for. He had hardly poked his ugly, devil nose outside the gate, when Thirty caught it in the coal tongs and squeezed and squeezed until tears flowed from the Devil's eyes.

'Hand over a sack of gold!' Thirty ordered. The wretched Devil stamped his hoof on the ground and straight away a sack of gold stood before him.

'What are you going to do with it? You'll never carry it,' said the Devil scornfully.

'Who said I'd carry it?' Thirty laughed. He ordered the Devil to load the sack on to the bed, while he lay there as well. Then he caught the Devil's tail in the tongs, and ordered him to pull the bed along.

The Devil pulled for all he was worth, and before long they were back at the farm. The farmer was thunderstruck, and Thirty could barely stop laughing.

'The sack of gold is mine, for I've won it. You keep the Devil as a farmhand,' he said and he threw the sack of gold over his shoulder as though it were a pillow full of feathers, and set off for home. From then on, no one in Thirty's family was ever in need. They did not mind at all that the gold came from the Devil's treasury. Indeed, whoever drinks tea brewed from mullein is not even afraid of Hell. As for the farmer, whatever he did, he could not chase the Devil off his farm.

The King Donkey and the Donkey King

A knight stepped from the shadows. His armour was dusty and dull, but he wore his helmet with its crest of blue flowers proudly. Little Pansy carelessly touched his spiked cloak.

'Ow, that hurts!' she cried and quickly pushed her little stinging finger into her mouth.

'I am Thistle and that is why I am prickly,' the spiky wanderer smiled, and began to tell his tale.

Beyond nine mountains and nine rivers a kingdom once lay. In that kingdom ruled a king the like of which the world has perhaps never known elsewhere. He was the biggest fool ever. Day after day, he issued laws to stagger the mind.

'I, your majesty the king, command all my subjects to gather the stars that fall from the skies at night and hand them in to the royal treasury. That is my law and it is in force from now on,' the foolish king proclaimed one morning. Another time he took it into his head to make another ridiculous proclamation. 'I command by my royal will and authority that my cold immediately leave me!' As we all know, a cold cannot be ordered about like that, and so the king commanded his subjects to sneeze and complain instead of him. He was such a stupid

man! People had had enough of this dunderhead's rule, but what can a poor man do against such a powerful ruler?

Once the king was walking through the castle garden, racking his brains to think up a new law for the benefit of his subjects. All this thinking made his throat dry, so he turned towards a nearby fountain to quench his thirst. All of a sudden, a stray donkey appeared. He was also thirsty. He ambled up to the fountain and was just about to dip his muzzle into the crystal water.

'Hey, wait a minute, knave!' the king interrupted the donkey. 'That would be a fine state of affairs for the ruler to have to give way to an ordinary animal. You ass, are you not aware in

whose presence you stand? I, your majesty the king, will be the first to drink,' and he pushed past the donkey and lowered his head to drink.

The donkey had not had the best upbringing in the world and the king's majesty meant nothing at all to him. It did not even occur to him to get out of the way. He butted the royal head until the king saw stars. Greatly angered, the king butted the donkey back with all his strength. A fight broke out. The king and the donkey fought each other like two cockerels on a dunghill. They thrust and pushed and butted their heads together until the sound echoed throughout the garden, for neither wanted to give in.

'The wisest one gives way, your highness,'

said a voice behind them. It was a frail little old woman but in reality, she was a magic fairy in disguise.

'For me to do that, I should have to turn into a donkey and the donkey into a king,' the ruler shouted.

The fairy laughed. 'As you wish, foolish king,' she said and was gone.

The king wanted to attack his rival again, but what had happened? Instead of a donkey, the king himself stood before him. 'But that's me,' he wanted to cry out, but all that came out was a helpless braying. He looked into the fountain and stopped in his tracks. Reflected in the water was the head of a donkey with great big donkey ears. 'Oh, no! I've turned into a donkey!' he moaned.

The donkey wasn't in any better state. He examined his noble robes with astonishment and upset, bit into a thistle. 'Ow, that hurts!' he cried in a human voice and kicked up his feet in a temper. Just then the animal's owner, an old vegetable grower, came along. When he saw the king, he was so frightened his knees trembled. The king was down on all fours, chewing thistles and kicking up his back legs like a donkey and beside him stood a donkey on its hind legs as though it had always walked like that. The animal brayed forlornly. Aghast, the vegetable grower fell to his knees.

'Please forgive me, your majesty,' he begged. 'My donkey is stupid and disobedient. He is always wandering off. I'll have to beat some sense into his head.'

'Did you call me stupid?' the ruler-donkey was offended.

'Oh no, your highness. I was speaking of the donkey,' the shocked vegetable grower declared.

'That's the point,' grumbled the bewitched donkey. The vegetable grower didn't wish to wait around any longer. He caught the bogus

/ 100 /

donkey by its yoke and jumped up on to its back. On the way home he beat it unmercifully with a stick. 'Just you wait. I'll give you what you deserve for wandering off,' he bellowed and he beat the animal until it was covered in bruises.

'You stupid lout, don't you recognize your king? Help, help, somebody! This murderer will go to the gallows!' the bewitched king cried in despair, but instead of a human voice, a donkey's bray came from his mouth. What a journey that was! By the time they reached the vegetable grower's garden, the king-donkey was almost on his last legs.

Meanwhile, in the palace, a search had been mounted for the king. A gardener came running in, quite dumbfounded. 'Good people, where are you? The king is running around the park on all fours. He is eating grass and chewing on branches,' he called. Everybody hurried outside and saw that the gardener was right. The courtiers were astounded. When they recovered a little, they bowed deeply to the king and spoke to him respectfully.

'Do forgive our impertinence, your majesty, but green grass will make your stomach ache. Please do not upset the royal tummy. There is a feast of the most select dishes set out for you in the palace. Please allow us to escort you to the table.'

The king, who was really the donkey, made no objections and allowed himself to be seated

at the table. He did not touch the numerous delicacies, however; instead, he began chewing his own slipper. Before anyone could stop him, he had devoured the sole. When the shocked courtiers had managed with great effort to get the king on his throne, it did not occur to him to issue new laws. He just nodded his head at everyone and when any question was put to him he retorted irritably, 'Can't you all leave me alone? Don't you see I am a donkey?'

To top it all, when evening came he would not go to the royal bed, but settled down instead on a bundle of straw in the stable.

People began to talk behind his back, saying, 'It is true. He is behaving like a donkey, but it seems he is wiser than he used to be. At least, he is not poking his nose into everything.'

So it went on day after day. The vegetable grower wasn't getting on any better, either. His donkey was making as much fuss as if he were the king himself. As soon as his wife put a meal on the table, the donkey was already there, and grabbing all the best bits. Then when evening came, the vegetable grower was looking forward to a rest at the end of his busy day, but he was out of luck. The donkey was lounging in his bed, helping himself to his snuff and reading an old book through his spectacles. He tried in vain to beat some sense into the donkey, but to no avail.

'Well, that's just about the limit,' the vegetable grower cried angrily one day when he caught the donkey in a corner trying to kiss his wife. 'Get out of my house, you wicked creature!' he cried, taking a whip to the donkey who took to his heels. He ran straight to the royal garden to get himself a cooling drink at the fountain. He had just bent his head to the water when along came the real donkey, who was still in the guise of the king. He, too, wished to drink at the fountain.

'Oh well, donkey, you are now my king and I, the king, am only an ordinary donkey so I must give way to you,' the king sighed, 'for the wisest one gives way.' With that, he changed again into the king and the false king changed back into

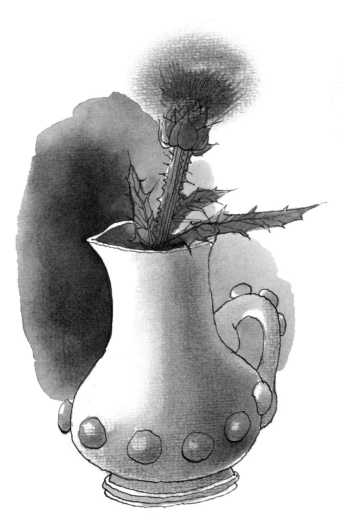

the donkey. The happy ruler immediately set out for the castle, resumed his seat on the throne and once more proclaimed a new law.

'I, his majesty the king, command that from this day on, a donkey must not be king and the king must not be a donkey.'

This was the first sensible law which had ever occurred to the ruler. From that time, the ruler had truly grown wise – but every day he insisted on having a thistle in the vase on his table. Perhaps this was so that he would never forget the time when he was really a proper donkey.

Bukur and his Children

'I want to hear something that frightens me a little!' declared the Rose Queen, looking around the ballroom.

'What about a dragon story?' asked the Field Poppy, who was quite red in the face from dancing.

'Why not?' Rose Queen agreed, 'but it must also make me laugh!' So the Field Poppy began his story. This is how it went.

There was much ado in the village the day Bukur and Mara were married. They were both poor as church mice, but even a poor person must dress up for such an occasion. So Bukur borrowed his wedding clothes from the scarecrow in the field and Mara sewed a veil from an old sack and because they had only one pair of clogs between them, Bukur took the left one and Mara the right and off they went to church. What a clatter they made as they marched along. They took with them the black billy goat and the white nanny as witnesses.

The priest gave them his blessing, Bukur and Mara gave each other a kiss, the two goats did their witnessing by bleating in harmony and off they all went.

When a man gets married, it stands to reason that he and his wife are not going to sleep out in the open, so Bukur and Mara started to build their own cottage. They decided to build their dwelling out of turf. It turned out a bit crooked, it is true, first leaning to the left then again to the right, a little bit forward and then a little bit backward. In short, it was a zigzag cottage. Bukur and Mara loved their little cottage, but whenever they looked at it from the outside, they burst out laughing.

'In time we will be lonely here on our own,' the wise Bukur said to Mara one day. 'Tell me, dear little wife, how many children do you want?'

'A whole crowd of them,' laughed Mara. 'Boys and girls in a row. As many as I give you kisses now,' she said and started giving Bukur so many kisses that he could barely count them all.

'Ninety-nine kisses,' he declared to his wife.

'Oh no, no. A full hundred,' Mara guessed.

'I tell you, it was ninety-nine,' Bukur insisted.

'I tell you one hundred,' Mara haggled.

Bukur sighed. 'Do you know what, Mara! We won't quarrel. We'll start again.' So they started once more and when at last they counted to one hundred, they hugged each other and danced for joy.

'That's it! We'll have an even one hundred children!' they said with glee.

As the years went by, however, no children came. Bukur was sad. He had a wife, he had a cottage, even his own little plot of land, but the children he and Mara wanted so much just never came. Bukur trudged around. He took care of his crops and in the middle of the golden wheat he saw the red of the field poppies and the blue of the beautiful cornflower, but they brought him no pleasure. Then one day Bukur noticed the flowers of the field poppies had gone and in their place green poppy heads had grown. The poppy heads ripened and Bukur was even sadder. Then, one day, as he sat at the edge of the field thinking sadly about the future, he heard tiny voices coming from one of the poppy heads.

'Let us out, Bukur,' they called.

'What on earth is this?' said Bukur in surprise. He carefully broke off the poppy head, took it home and opened it with a knife. Poppy seeds poured from the poppy head, and hardly had they fallen to the ground than each one of them turned into a little child. The boys were like little elves and the girls were like little fairies. Altogether, there were exactly one hundred. In all the excitement Bukur and Mara only just managed to count them. Suddenly it was like a village fair in the cottage. The boys ran in all directions, exploring every corner and climbing up the chimney on to the roof. They jumped into Mara's washtub and clambered into Bukur's trousers. They fenced with knitting needles and pulled their sisters' hair until the poor girls squeeled like little pigs. Bukur and Mara laughed and laughed with joy.

'Well, Mara, at last we have got what we wanted,' Bukur said when they had laughed their fill. 'Now it will be up to me to feed all those little ones somehow. Our little field will not be enough for that. I will have to go out into the world to look for work.'

He put a slice of bread in one pocket and lump of curd cheese in the other and off he went. After some time he bumped into some shepherds. They sat in silence around a little fire, staring gloomily at the flames.

'Ho good shepherds, why are you so sad? If I had such a fine flock of sheep I'd be singing for joy.'

'If it were as simple as that, we'd be singing, too,' replied the shepherds. 'In a short while a dragon will be coming for our flock. Every day we have to bring him a fresh lot of sheep or he will destroy us. Soon we will have no sheep left.'

'Something will have to be done about that,' Bukur said crossly. 'Such lovely sheep are too good for the jaws of a dragon. Half of that flock would be enough for me to feed my little ones all the year round. If you promise to give me half and we drive them to my cottage, then somehow I will deal with the dragon.'

The shepherds promised and as Buker desired they gathered the sheep from the slopes and drove them to the cottage. Mara was overjoyed. Meanwhile, Bukur sat on a rock, blowing on his long shepherd's pipe loudly enough to make anyone deaf and tending the old ram left behind by the shepherds. Just then, the dragon appeared! He had three heads and flames shot forth out of each of his mouths.

'Where are my sheep,' he roared till the trees shook.

'What's that about something cheap?' Bukur said putting his hand to his ear as though he couldn't hear.

'Sheep, I say,' thundered the dragon.

'Yes, it is a nice day,' Bukur grinned.

'Talking to you is like talking to a brick wall!' the dragon roared in anger. 'If you don't give me my sheep this very moment I'll eat you in one gulp,' he raged.

'I beat you,' Bukur replied. 'Why don't you speak up, you whippersnapper? I can hardly hear you. If you want to try your strength against me, why not show me first how strong you are. Squeeze a stone in your claws until water runs from it. If you can't do that, then it would be pointless for us to fight. I could kill you!'

The dragon snatched up the nearest stone, squeezed it and crushed it to pieces, but not a drop of water fell from it.

'You jellyfish,' Bukur scowled. 'Look what I can do.' Reaching quickly into his pocket, Bukur pulled out the lump of curd cheese and squeezed it until the whey ran out.

'That's nothing either,' Bukur boasted. 'I have a hundred children at home. They are so small they can all fit into a single poppy head together, but each of them is a hundred times stronger than I am.'

The dragon was terrified. 'I say, I don't mean any harm, brother,' he said, trying to humour Bukur. 'Why don't you come into my service? If you serve me for one year I'll reward you well.'

'How long is a dragon's year?' Bukur asked.

'Three whole days,' replied the dragon.

Bukur objected. 'That's an awfully long time, but to oblige you, we'll shake on it,' and so they did. The dragon led Bukur to his den where his old dragon wife was waiting with the fire already made.

'Where are the sheep?' she asked.

'For today we must be content with one ram. Instead, I have brought you a servant who is as strong as an ox,' and he quickly whispered into his wife's ear what feats of strength Bukur was capable of. The suspicious dragon wife took her husband aside.

'You are a fool,' she said. 'If he is really as strong as all that, then we must find a trick to get rid of him or he'll kill both of us. When he is asleep at night, you must strike him three times on his head with your stick.'

Bukur acted as though he was taking no notice of them but he heard every word. That

night, when they all went to bed, he crept silently to the wood pile, and picking up a big piece of oak wood, crept back and put it into his bed. The dragon woke up in the night, took up his huge stick and with all his strength, struck three times where Bukur should have had his head. 'That's the end of him,' he said to his wife, got back into bed and went to sleep. What a surprise they got when they opened their eyes in the morning and saw Bukur, sitting on his bed and yawning.

'I slept badly last night,' Bukur complained. 'A flea bit my forehead three times in the night.'

The dragon and his wife grew pale with fear. When they had gathered their wits together, the dragon said, 'Take my stick outside and throw it up into the crown of the pine tree. We need to knock down a few cones to light the fire.'

'All right,' Bukur agreed, 'But I don't know how to control my strength. What if your cudgel should fly somewhere up to the moon? My brother is a blacksmith there and he would never return it to you. He is an old miser.'

'Oh goodness!' the dragon cried in horror.

'That stick is made of pure gold. I'd rather shake the pine-cones down myself.' So he set to work and Bukur lay in the grass doing nothing until the evening. That first day of service passed pleasantly to be sure.

The next day the dragon decided that they would go together to the well to carry water, so they took two huge water bags and off they went. Bukur wasn't about to tell the dragon, but he was almost crushed under the weight of the empty water bag.

When the dragon had filled his bag, he made room for Bukur. 'It's your turn now. Let your bag down into the well.' Instead, Bukur took his knife and started to dig into the earth around the well.

'What are you doing?' the dragon asked.

'What do you think I'm doing? I'm digging up the well. I'll carry it on my back to the cave. I'm certainly not going to trouble myself by coming to the well every day,' Bukur laughed. The dragon was aghast.

'Oh please don't do that. It might damage the spring. I'd rather carry the water myself.' When they returned to the cave, the dragon told his wife what terrific strength Bukur had and she was so shocked she almost burned the pancakes on the stove.

On the third day the dragon took Bukur to the forest to collect firewood. He pulled up one pine tree after another and threw them over his shoulder. Meanwhile, Bukur made out he was going to wind a rope around the forest.

'What are you up to now?' said the dragon a little annoyed.

'What do you think I'm doing? I am tying up the whole forest into a bundle. I'm going to take it in one go. I am certainly not going to trudge all the way here and back every day just for a little firewood.'

'Stop that, you fool!' shouted the dragon in a fury. 'Do you want to lay waste the whole forest? I'd rather carry the firewood myself.'

Puffing and blowing, the dragon set off back to the cave and Bukur strolled after him at a leisurely pace.

'Look here, Bukur,' said the dragon and his wife when Bukur got back. 'Your year of service is over, take a sack of gold pieces and off you go. Let us not see you ever again!'

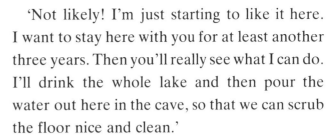

'Not likely! I'm just starting to like it here. I want to stay here with you for at least another three years. Then you'll really see what I can do. I'll drink the whole lake and then pour the water out here in the cave, so that we can scrub the floor nice and clean.'

'You can't do that to us, Bukur,' the dragons wailed. 'You are a good-natured man but we shall manage somehow without your service. Instead, why don't you take three sacks of gold and just leave us in peace.'

'Perhaps you are right,' Bukur smiled, 'but I am all worn out from that service. I'll just rest here for another dragon year.'

'Oh no, not that,' the dragon implored. 'I'll carry those sacks home for you myself. Just go back to where you came from.' The dragon loaded himself with the gold, Bukur sat on his tail and they were off. Oh my! What a ride it was! The dragon panted and snorted, Bukur sang merrily and people an all sides waved to him. When he arrived at the cottage, Bukur's children poured out like a swarm of bees, all shouting and cheering.

'Why is your family making such a row?' the dragon scowled.

'Well, it's because they are hungry,' Bukur chuckled. 'They are hoping for a dragon roast.'

When the dragon heard this, he dropped the sacks of gold and Bukur with them and fled, never to be seen again in those parts.

So at last Bukur and Mara found pleasure in their children and in the wealth they had gained. It was enough to last for the whole of their lives and there was still some left over for others. Bukur happily surveyed his land and Mara told fairytales to the children. Her favourite was the one about the poppy seeds and she told it to each of her children at least one hundred times.

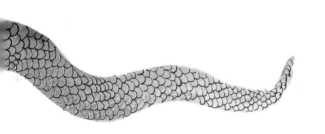

Cowslip's Tale

A prince dressed in yellow bowed and introduced himself. 'My name is Cowslip,' he said. 'Legend has it that Saint Peter once lost the keys to the Gates of Heaven. They dropped from star to star until they hit the ground. The angels found them and gathered them up, but lovely yellow flowers sprang from where they had fallen. They cannot open the Gates of Heaven but, each year, they unlock the gate for spring to enter. They also open the way to hidden treasures. Listen.'

There were once three brothers. They lived in a tumbledown cottage and want was as natural to them as water is to a fish. The heart of the youngest of them, Georgie, was not hardened by this poor life. He was kind and generous and would have given even the little he had to the needy. The older brothers were proper skinflints, however, and it's a wonder they survived their own envy and malice.

One day in autumn, the eldest of the brothers took his little goat out for the last time to graze the sparse grass. It was as cold as in the middle of January, the sky lowering with snow, and so the wretched fellow huddled close to his small fire and complained about the whole world.

Just then, however, he caught sight of a little yellow flower.

'Look at that, a cowslip!' he gasped. 'Where did it come from in autumn?' He did not wonder for long, though. He picked the flower and slipped it into his hatband. When the little

/ 110 /

goat had grazed her fill, he chased her hurriedly home. On the way, his hat got heavier and heavier as if it were made of lead. The poor man took off his hat and stared in surprise. Instead of the cowslip, a large gold key was stuck in the hatband! At that same moment his little goat turned into a lovely fair-skinned girl. Only her goat horns still peeped from her golden hair. She smiled mysteriously at the eldest brother and beckoned him to follow her. He went after her as though he were bewitched. After a while the girl brought him to a large hill made of solid gold, with a little keyhole at its foot.

'Maa-aa,' the goat-girl bleated. 'You grazed me well. In return you may open this hill, which is full of treasures. Listen what I say, however! Don't leave the most valuable thing behind!' After speaking these words, the girl vanished. The poor fellow lost no time and thrust the gold key into the keyhole. The hill opened up with a blinding flash and he found himself in the centre of a large cave full of gold coins, silver goblets, pearls and precious jewels. Such treasure! The greedy brother did not know what to go for first. When he could get nothing more into his pockets or under his shirts he raced home with his riches.

'I'll come back again, anyway,' he decided, but the moment he left the cave, the hill closed with a crash behind him. It was then he realized that he had left behind in the cave the most valuable thing – the gold key.

'Oh well, I shan't suffer poverty for the rest of my life and, whenever I want, I can dig a fine tunnel into the golden hill,' he said to himself, and went off to the village. He did not go back to his two brothers, for he did not want to share his treasures with them. He bought a fine house and lived like a gentleman from then on, doing no work and eating only the best food. His

clothes were better than a duke's and he had parties galore, inviting all the best people. Before long, the last gold coin had gone from his pocket. In direst poverty he set out for the golden hill, but it had vanished from the face of the earth. In the end, the unfortunate fellow had to sell his fine house, and because it was against his nature to work, he had soon spent every last penny. He had no choice but to go back begging to his brothers.

Time passed swiftly and one autumn day, the middle brother set out to graze his ewe. Winter was about to begin and all the grass was brown and withered. Still, the ewe enjoyed her grazing, but the miserable brother crouched beside his small fire and grumbled at his fate. Suddenly, in front of him a little flower appeared.

'Well, just look at that, a cowslip! Where did it come from so close to winter?' the poor fellow marvelled. Pleased, he tucked it into his hatband. On the way home the flower turned into a silver key. As the poor man was staring at it in disbelief, a fair-haired girl appeared before him in place of his ewe. She called to him, and after a while brought him to a silver hill with a keyhole at its foot. He wasted no time and hurried to open the hill with his silver key.

'Baa-aa,' bleated the sheep-girl. 'Because you grazed me so well, I'll give you some advice. Take as much gold and precious stones as you can carry, but don't forget the most valuable thing.' Then she vanished.

The middle brother ignored her words. He grabbed what he could and rushed home, forgetting to take the silver key with him. Like his brother before him, he did not know how to make best use of his riches, however, and was soon penniless.

So the three brothers were worse off than ever. When the weather struck cold the follow-ing year, the youngest brother, Georgie, set out for a walk in the forest. On his shoulder he carried his beloved white dove.

'Perhaps I'll find something to feed you at least,' he comforted her and when they reached a pine grove, he picked the seeds from cones and broke open long-forgotten nuts from the hazel bushes for his little bird to peck. Just then something yellow glistened on the snow.

'My goodness me, a cowslip!' Georgie cried in amazement. 'Why, it's a long time to spring.' At once, he placed the flower in his hatband as a fine ornament, but as he walked, the hat got heavier and heavier. With surprise, Georgie found that the flower had turned into a large glass key. At that, the little dove settled at his feet and turned into a girl. Instead of hair, she had white feathers on her head. She called to him and Georgie followed her as though bewitched. Before long, they arrived at a glass hill. The girl told Georgie to open the hill with the glass key.

'You have taken good care of me, Georgie,' she said. 'I will reward you. Inside is a cave full of treasures but, if you want to be happy, take from there only what is most valuable.' Then she vanished.

Georgie went along a glass corridor into the cave. It was full of crystal vases and, in each vase, silver and gold cowslips were blooming, while all around shone gold and precious stones. On a little glass table in a corner of the cave stood a small glass statue of a girl. She was so beautiful that Georgie could not take his eyes off her. He cared for nothing else, took the little table and the statue and set out for home with a merry song on his lips, with no thought for the glass key.

'You chose well, Georgie,' the statue said and turned into a lovely girl. 'If you had taken the

glass key, I should have run away from you, back into the glass hill. You would never have found me again. If you had gathered up armfuls of treasure, it would not have brought you happiness. Thank you for delivering me from an evil magic spell. If you want me to, I will marry you.'

How could Georgie not want her to! As long as the world had existed, no one had ever seen such beauty. He joyfully put his arm around the girl's waist, hoisted the little table on to his shoulder and set out for his cottage. His elder brothers were dumbstruck, even more so when Georgie stood the little glass table in the middle of the room. Suddenly a meal fit for a king spread upon it. In each corner, there was a gold

coin. Georgie shared everything honestly with his brothers and his lovely wife did her fair share of work around the house. The glass table always provided them with delicacies and there was a gold coin for each of them after the meal.

Poverty left the little cottage, but even so, the elder brothers were consumed with envy. One day, they plotted together and decided to steal the little glass table. When Georgie and his wife were sleeping that night, the brothers crept out of the cottage with it and started to run away. They didn't get far, however, before they began to squabble over the table. They pulled and pushed and dragged the little table over the rough ground, until it shattered into a thousand glass splinters. With very bad feeling between them, the two brothers went off, each in a different direction, to look for more cowslip keys. I don't think they've found one yet, as they still have not returned.

In the morning, when Georgie saw what had happened, he was sad, but his wife comforted him, 'Don't be upset, Georgie. We can still make a living by working hard.'

'You are right, dear wife,' Georgie smiled, and so Georgie and his wife lived on there happily and if they have not died, they will be living there to this day.

The Sprig
of Heather

A rose-coloured fairy danced before the throne. She muttered a swift greeting to the Rose Queen and at once started chasing an unruly little will-o'-the-wisp.

'Who are you?' the Rose Queen frowned.

'It's me,' the girl replied flippantly, but when she realized that the Queen was really cross, she added, 'I am the little fairy from a sprig of heather. Please don't be angry with me. I'll tell you a nice story.'

Far, far away — it could have been right at the end of the world, a lonely little hut stood in the middle of a barren wasteland. A poor widow lived in this little hut, with her son Jack. An endless carpet of heather, bare rocks and treacherous bogs stretched as far as the eye could see. People found life harsh here, but fairies, will-o'-the-wisps and all sorts of other magical beings got on well in this mysterious land. Jack used to listen to the stories his mother told about them and he would have given almost anything for just one of those little fairies to wander into their home so that he could have someone to play with. Jack was often lonely. When darkness began to fall over the countryside, he would sit at the window and gaze longingly towards the bog where flashing will-o'-the-wisps, rainbow flames and strange glowing rings would appear. Jack knew that they were the skirts of dancing fairies and he could not keep his eyes off them. In vain his mother urged him to go to bed, but it was as though he could not hear her.

'If you don't do what I say, the will-o'-the-wisps will come for you and take you off to the bog,' said Mummy once. 'Hurry to bed, you rascal! The will-o'-the-wisps and the fairies can't come after you there.' Jack didn't wait around and soon he was cuddled up under the blankets. Do you think he was afraid of the will-o'-the-wisps? What nonsense!

The moment Mummy was asleep, the little boy slipped out of bed, tiptoed to the fireplace and raked the smouldering embers. Then he placed some dried heather sprigs on the fire. Sparks flew, the fire crackled, flames began to dance and there was a strange roaring in the chimney. Then the flames died down and an odd creature jumped out of the fireplace. Its hair glowed pink, its eyes had a rosy hue, and its

little skirt was a rose-coloured flame! It was a fairy! Smaller than a thumb, slimmer than a little finger and what beauty!

'Who are you?' Jack asked in wonder.

'I am me,' said the fairy and made a curtsy. 'And who are you?'

'Me too,' Jack replied. He had a feeling that this little sprite was making fun of him.

'That's a very nice name,' the little fairy giggled. 'Come and let me show you something,' she said enticingly. She bent over the fireplace and blew on the embers. Flames sprang up and, abracadabra, they turned into flamebirds, beetles, little animals, flowers and trees. Fiery butterflies danced over a fiery meadow and fiery swans floated on fiery lakes, while hunters in fiery clothes walked through

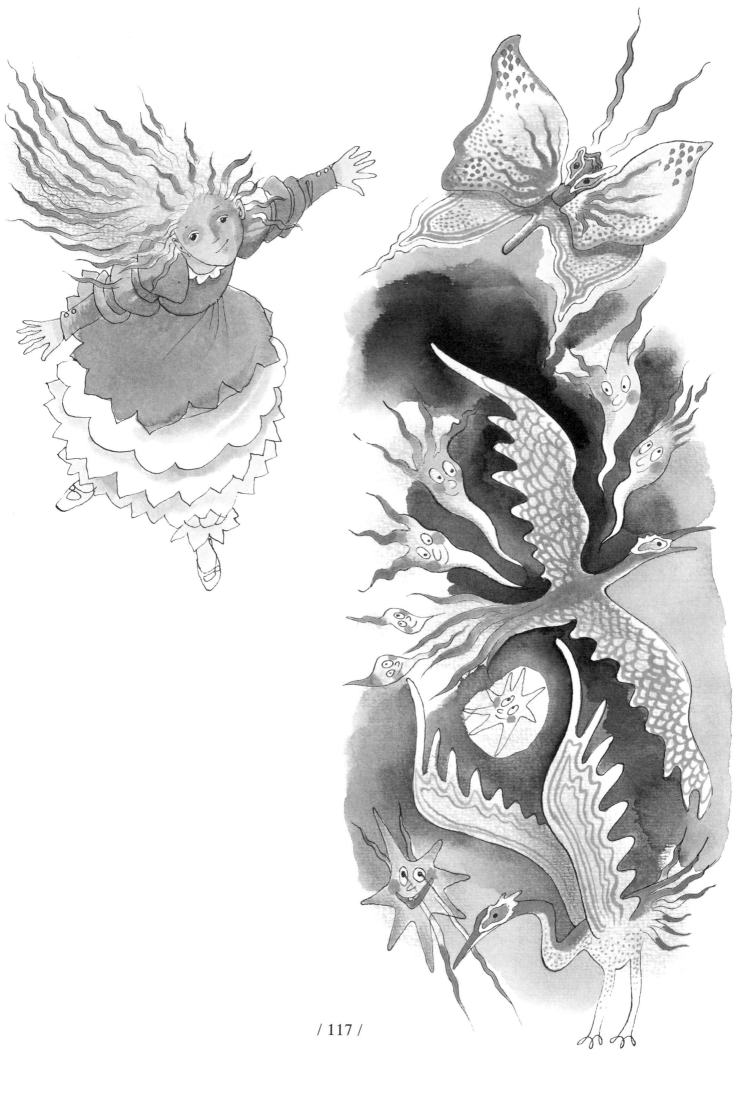

fiery forests. The fairy blew once again on the embers, the flames danced up obligingly and changed into fiery palaces full of fiery princes and princesses, court ladies and noble knights. They danced together on the glowing embers and fiery musicians played them fiery tunes.

Then everything vanished. Jack clapped his hands with joy. 'More, more!' he called, but the fairy did not want to blow on the embers a third time. So the boy bent down and blew himself. What happened! The flame leaped up, from the flame a spark and the spark fell right on to the satin slipper of the little fairy.

'Oh dear, oh dear!' the little creature shrieked, 'my slipper is burning.'

Suddenly, however, it was not the cry of a little girl any more. It moaned like the wind in

the chimney, it rumbled like a thunderstorm and it howled like a pack of wild animals. It seemed to Jack that all the monsters in the whole world were trying to get into the cottage. He clapped his hands over his ears in terror, but it did not help. The howling did not stop.

'Where can I hide? I know, I'll get into bed. Will-o'-the-wisps and awful fairies cannot go there.' As soon he thought of it, he was under the covers.

He could just about hear the strict voice of the mother fairy from the chimney. 'Who is crying?' she shouted, making soot fall down the chimney.

'It's me,' the little fairy whined. 'One of my slippers is burned.'

'Who did it to you?' mother fairy cried.

'I just fell over,' the little fairy girl answered, and under the covers Jack trembled.

The mother fairy let fly at the unfortunate creature. 'Then why are you calling on me for help, you clumsy thing? When you yourself are to blame, then it's you who have to put it right. Just wait. You'll pay dearly for this!'

Out of the corner of his eye and firmly tucked up in bed, Jack saw a long fiery arm reach out from the fireplace, catch the little fairy by the ear and pull her up the chimney. Well, well, there was so much wailing and complaining in the wind. Jack quickly pulled the blankets over his head so as not to hear, for will-o'-the-wisps and fairies were unable to reach him there. From that time on, his mother never needed to chase him to bed again. No more did he want to play with the fairies. What if one of them should tell the mother fairy his name? And what if she burned her slipper again? It was just too terrible to imagine!

Flowers of Gold

'My homeland is in the East. It is the country written about in *A Thousand and One Nights,*' said Prince Hyacinth, ringing his little bells as he bowed. 'The noble poet Hafiz used to sing about me when, on magical nights, moonlight nestled in the hair of young girls. Now people know me all over the world, and wherever I have been I have heard enchanting stories. Listen I'll tell you one now.'

A long, long time ago lived a man and woman who had only one son. Even from the time he was a small child, the boy was clever and wise and so his father was not surprised when one day his son said to him, 'Daddy, I am big enough to be able to help you make a living. Let me train as a goldsmith. I want to make beautiful flowers of gold.'

The old man decided to let his son learn the craft. He took his son to a friend who was a goldsmith and entrusted him to his care. The boy was a willing worker. Before long he was more skilful than the goldsmith himself and his young hands shaped the most beautiful jewellery. The most wonderful of all his creations were the flowers of gold which made the king himself stand in wonder.

One day, a Bedouin tribesman came to the workshop. He brought with him a basket of the most splendid red hyacinths.

'I have never seen such strange flowers before. They are truly beautiful,' the young man sighed. 'I want to make these flowers out of gold.'

The Bedouin smiled. 'There is no need, my son. Place my flowers in the fire for a few moments, then you will see something never seen by anyone else in the world.'

The young man was reluctant for he did not want to destroy such beauty, but when the stranger insisted, he consented. To his amazement in the fire the hyacinths changed into glowing flowers of rare red gold. The young man could not believe his eyes.

'Please tell me your secret, old man,' he begged. 'Where did you get such a magic bouquet?'

'Not where you would expect, young man,' the Bedouin answered. 'But because I like you, I'll tell you. Right in the middle of a vast desert, a very high mountain rises up to the clouds. There is an enormous garden on the top of the mountain. It is full of magical flowers. Old folk say that the garden belongs to the King of the Genies. It is said that their palace of dewdrops and rainbows stands somewhere hidden among the flowers, but no one has ever gone any further than the first bed of hyacinths. If you like, I will lead you to the mountain. You would never find the way yourself.'

Joyfully the young man agreed and early next morning he set of into the desert with his guide. They travelled for many miles and the young man was beginning to think that the Bedouin had lost his way, but then suddenly, in front of them, a mountain arose, as high as the sky, as smooth as glass and encircled by flying white eagles.

'We have arrived,' said the old man. 'When you are at the top, dig up an armful of the magic hyacinths for us to share. You will have to hurry though, in case the Genie Princesses catch you.'

'Alas, old man! I shall never reach the top of the mountain,' the young man lamented. 'The

rock is as slippery as an iceberg.' 'Don't worry young man,' said the Bedouin. 'I have brought a camel skin with me. I shall sew you into it and the white eagles will carry you high above the clouds to the top of the mountain.'

As the old man said, so it happened. When the eagles settled with their burden on the top of the mountain, the boy cut open the camel

skin and climbed out. All around grew thousands of flowers. The young man did not waste any time. He quickly gathered an armful of the red hyacinths and threw them down the mountain to the old man.

'How do I get down?' the young man called anxiously. From the foot of the mountain there came the sound of evil laughter.

'You foolish boy,' the old man sneered. 'You will never be able to get down. Thank you for the magical flowers, you stupid fellow! I wish you an early death.'

With these words, the treacherous man went on his way. The boy shook with fear, and looking down, saw human bones shining among the flowers. Frightened, the young man took to his heels and ran he knew not where. Suddenly he heard a voice cry out.

'If you are a good person, please help me,' called a young white eagle. His wing was caught

among thorny branches. The young goldsmith hurried to the thorn bush and freed the young eagle. Just then two gigantic white birds dropped from the skies, caught up the young man in their claws and carried him up into the clouds. The poor fellow fainted with fear, but when he came to his senses, he could not believe his eyes. He was lying on scented pillows in a splendid rainbow palace surrounded by seven beautiful dancing girls.

'Who are you and where am I?' the young man asked.

'We are the Genie Princesses. Our father is the King of the Genies,' the loveliest of them all replied. 'You are in our magical palace. No human has yet found the way to us, but you were brought to us by our faithful white eagles. You helped their baby bird and so in gratitude, they saved your life.'

The girls, all talking at once, asked the young man what he had been doing in their garden. The young man told them everything and said how the wily old man deceived him.

'We know that wicked fellow,' the lovely girls told him. 'Every year he brings some unfortunate person to our mountain. He tricks them into gathering the magical hyacinths from our garden. Bound by a spell in each of those flowers is one year of our lives. When these unlucky fellows have carried out their task, the old man leaves them to the mercy of the elements.'

The young goldsmith fell to his knees. 'Oh, please forgive me, Genie Princesses, I had no idea what the red hyacinths meant for you. It never occurred to me that with each flower, I was stealing a year of your lives.'

The girls laughed. 'Don't be upset, young man, there are thousands of our flowers just as there are thousands of years of our lives. One here or there is of little importance. We are still young,' said the loveliest princess. Evil must not go unpunished however. Stay here with us in the palace until that terrible man returns. Then you can kill him with our magic dagger.'

The young man was glad to stay. He had fallen in love with the most beautiful Princess and a year passed as in a sweet dream. One day, the beautiful princess spoke to him. 'The time has come for us to part. Your deceitful guide

has returned with another victim and is even now at the foot of the mountain. Take my dagger and bear this in mind. That old fellow is not an ordinary man. In his chest he carries the heart of his donkey and he keeps his own heart in the donkey's body. If you want to come out of this alive, then you must stab the old man's donkey.'

The young man said good-bye sadly. 'I love you,' he whispered.

The girl smiled. 'Remember your promise. Evil must be punished,' she said. Then she called the white eagle to her and ordered him to carry the boy to the foot of the mountain. When the old man saw the goldsmith, he grew pale with fear.

'I know that I should be punished for my evil deed. You have the right to take your revenge. So, thrust your dagger into my heart!' The young man was not tricked, however, and mindful of the instructions he had been given, he plunged the blade of the dagger into the body of the donkey. At that moment, the old man fell to the ground, dead. The goldsmith explained to the evil old man's victim what fate would have awaited him on top of the mountain and then together the two of them started the long journey home.

The boy's parents and the goldsmith's parents were all overjoyed at their return, but even though he was once again safe, the goldsmith was not happy. One day, there appeared a huge white eagle, in the sky. Seated on it, was the beautiful Genie Princess. In her arms she held a mass of red hyacinths.

Kneeling before the young man she whispered, 'I can't live without you. My noble father said I may come to you. Take these red hyacinths and change them in the fire to flowers of gold. They will make you rich. Only plant for

me enough living flowers in a garden to make up one human life. I don't want to live longer than you. I will be your faithful wife until we both die.'

So ends Prince Hyacinth's story. The goldsmith and his beloved wife lived a good and pleasant life. When the day came to mark the end of their time on earth and the last of the hyacinths in the young man's garden began to fade, the couple sat together at their door, holding hands and smiling.

Then high up in the heavens, the wings of

seven white eagles could be heard approaching. On their backs they carried the king of the Genies with his gentle daughters. They had come to say a last goodbye to the one who, for the love of a man, changed her immortality for the fleeting life of a human. In their sorrow they cried rainbow tears. People in the desert looked up to the sky with wonder and called to each other, 'Look, it's raining!', and on the rain was the sweet scent of hyacinths.

The Mountain Fairy

'My name is Edelweiss,' a countess in a snow-white fur jacket began. 'My tale comes from high up in the mountains just like I do!'

If you were to set out upstream along the Silver river you would reach a very high range of mountains. Long, long ago these mountains were bleak and desolate. Sadness dwelled in this realm of silent rocks. No grass grew there and no flowers opened their petals to please the eye and gladden the heart. The ruler there was an old king with a white beard and a snow-white moustache and whose one delight was his beautiful daughter. She was born of a clear

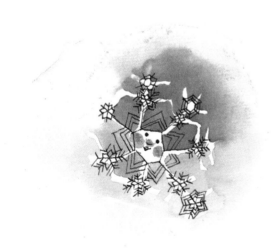

mountain spring, as are all the mountain fairies, and before she was able to walk, she slept in a cot made of ice. She did not look like an ordinary princess either. She was as transparent as water and she sparkled like a crystal fountain. When she smiled, the sky glowed rosy and when she cried, snowflakes fell from her eyes.

The fairy liked to wander through the still, silent snow-covered mountain kingdom. From high above she could look longingly down into the valleys where flowers of every colour and scent grew. One day she could not resist any longer and floated down like a snow cloud into

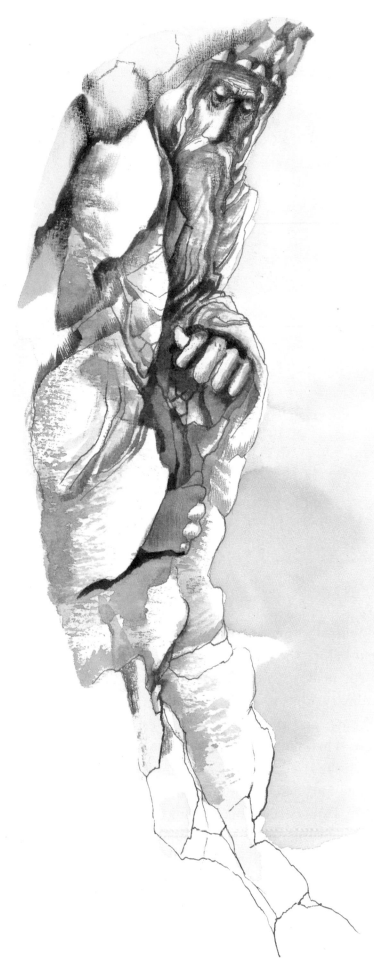

a meadow where she gathered an armful of meadow flowers. She wanted to plant them beneath the windows of her palace in a garden of snow, but the flowers could not stand her frozen embrace or the old king's icy breath. The poor flowers wilted and froze and the fairy was so sad she cried snowflake tears over them.

From then on she did not dare to touch a single green leaf. She sat wistfully in the cold palace and breathed icy flowers on the windows. They were beautiful but they had no life.

So the fairy sat, day after day, crying as though her heart were about to break. The sound of her crying reached the ears of a charcoal burner's daughter who lived in the meadow. Her mother had told her the story of the mountain fairy and she was very sad at the thought of the lonely ice princess.

'Father, mother,' she begged one day. 'Come out into the meadow with me to ask the little wild flowers to go up to the mountain kingdom to see the mountain fairy.

Her parents were glad to do what their daughter asked. They all held hands and wandered from flower to flower, from marsh marigold to cowslip, from forget-me-not to daisy, begging and pleading with the flowers, but it was no use. The flowers were afraid of the cold mountain winds, the frost and the everlasting snow which covered the ground, and did not dare to go to the mountain kingdom lest they freeze to death. The little girl cried bitterly. Just then, a fragile little white flower, the Edelweiss, peeped out of the moss.

'Why are you crying?' Edelweiss asked the little girl, and the little girl told Edelweiss about the lonely mountain fairy. Edelweiss was touched by the story and promised that she would go up into the mountains to the palace of the silver-headed king and his daughter. She did as she promised, and taking leave of all her flower sisters in the meadow, set out for the frozen kingdom.

The charcoal burner's daughter called out joyfully, 'Mountain fairy, mountain fairy, I am sending little white Edelweiss to you to cheer up your icy heart.'

The little girl's call was heard by Echo who passed it on from rock to rock until the message came to the ear of the icy princess. Wasting no time she made a little white fur coat from hoar frost and star fluff, and when at last the weary Edelweiss climbed over a granite rock to reach the highest chalk cliff, the fairy placed her in a little sheltered crack in the rock. So that she would not be cold, she wrapped her in the little velvety coat. Edelweiss was soon happy up in the mountains. She was close to the sun and the stars, white clouds floated around her and the gentle mist went to sleep in her flowers. She felt as though she were in heaven.

When the rest of the flowers in the valley heard how well Edelweiss was getting on high in the mountains, they plucked up courage and gradually crept up the mountain after her. Phlox went with primrose, then cowslip and gentian, autumm crocus, knot-grass and saxif- rage, bryony and snakeroot and many others. Some of them nestled under rocks, others settled on the borders of streams and yet others climbed up higher and higher, some right up to little Edelweiss.

At last the fairy princess was happy. She was busy from morning till evening, taking care that the flowers did not wither. At night she closed their petals and in the long evenings she wove soft carpets from clove pinks. It was always Edelweiss she loved best of all however, and would stroke the little white flowers as she thought of the charcoal burner's daughter.

When winter came the fairy cried soft snow beds for the flowers so that frost's long icy fingers would not reach their roots, and she looked forward to the spring. One cold winter, though, Echo brought to the mountain fairy the sound of a child crying. It was the charcoal burner's daughter who had suddenly fallen ill. She grew pale and wasted away little by little as the days went by. Not even the village doctor could help her. The mountain fairy flew to the charcoal burner's cottage and watched through the window as the little girl lay in bed with her mother and father kneeling at her bed side.

The little girl spoke and the mountain fairy heard her words. 'I miss the flowers,' the little voice said. 'If I don't see flowers through the window today, I shall die.'

The charcoal burner and his wife hung their heads. 'Where can we find flowers in the winter time?' they sobbed.

With that, the mountain fairy crept nearer and nearer and with her icy breath made flowers appear on the window. Lifeless as they were, they were beautiful and when the little girl saw them she began to smile. From that moment she hardly ever stopped smiling and when the spring spread a carpet of brightly coloured flowers across the meadow, the little girl went to the cottage door and called to the mountains, 'Thank you, thank you, mountain fairy.'

From somewhere high above the valley an answer came.

'Thank you, thank you, thank you.'

Johnnie the Hunchback

Suddenly, up popped a sweet-scented girl, covered in small flowers. Breathless from dancing, she began her tale.

Once upon a time there was a king, and this king had three daughters. The first daughter had a big nose, the second had big ears and the third was covered in freckles. Altogether, in the eyes of the king they were quite beautiful. The first could count to one, the second to two and the third to three. Altogether thought the king they were quite smart. The youngest squinted, the middle one was hard of hearing and the eldest was lame in both legs. Altogether they were as sound in health as a bell. The king was very proud of his daughters and took even greater care of them than of his own long beard. They were never allowed out without great numbers of guards and gold coins for sweets.

One day, the princesses went out for a trip in a gold carriage. They were followed by 777 knights, 777 ladies-in-waiting and 777 cooks and kitchen helps and, to make up the number, one skinny little dwarf who finished up the leftovers. This dwarf was called Johnnie and he had two humps, one in the front and one at the back. During the journey he turned somer-

saults, sang amusing songs and talked a lot of nonsense just to keep the princesses entertained. He really did keep them laughing fit to burst. The youngest one pulled a face at him and then winked, first with one eye and then the other. She liked Johnnie very much. She would have quite liked to be his girlfriend, but Johnnie was in love with Mathilda the kitchen maid, who was also in love with him.

Suddenly, without warning, a giant stepped into the path of the carriage. His head was somewhere above the clouds and on the head, instead of a hat, was a stone tower. He stood fanning his face with a huge pine tree to keep the flies away and when he was thirsty he drank water from the rain clouds.

When the knights saw him, they drew their golden swords, raised their silver lances and their 777 voices called as one man, 'Out of the way, out of the way, you bold fool! The royal princesses are in the carriage. If you do not make way, you are done for!'

They at once started to cut and thrust at the giant's foot until it was covered in pinpricks. Angered, the giant shuffled his feet, almost causing the streams to break their banks.

'Thunder and lightning,' he growled. 'I've stepped into an ants' nest again!' and he sneezed so hard that an awful hurricane blew over the whole land. The hurricane scattered the royal procession on all sides. Only the carriage did not fly away, it being made of gold and too heavy.

'Today of all days there had to be such a wind,' grumbled the princesses. 'It'll put our hair into a proper tangle.'

Just then, the giant noticed something glittering at his feet. He bent down and lifted the gold carriage up into the clouds. 'Well look at this,' he said joyfully when he saw the princesses sitting in the carriage. 'Three charming little dolls, for me to play with.' So that the carriage with the young girls would not slip through his fingers, he put it under his hat. The princesses then found themselves imprisoned in the stone tower on his head.

What happened next? Well it was like this. The wind scattered all the knights and ladies-in-waiting like dandelion fluff. They never found their way home again and to this day are still wandering somewhere in the world. Only our dear little Johnnie was blown by the wind right back to the royal castle.

'How are my beloved daughters, the princesses, getting on?' the king asked. When the king heard what had happened to the princesses, he tore his venerable beard in despair until there was nothing of it left on his chin. At once he made a proclamation to the whole world that he would give his kingdom to the one who would bring them back.

'That would suit me down to the ground,' Johnnie Hunchback thought and straight away informed his mother that he was setting out to free the princesses from the giant's clutches.

'Take a rope and bucket with you,' the wise woman told her son. 'Drink water from all the wells you come across but don't touch anything else or you will have no strength.'

Johnnie obeyed and went out into the world. He went where his feet carried him and when he was too weak to go on, he took water from a well and his strength returned. So he travelled from well to well. At one of them, though, his bucket became untied from the rope and dropped into the water. What could Johnnie do but climb down for it. A little stone glittered at the bottom of the well.

'Good day, Johnnie,' the little stone said. 'What do you want here?' Johnnie told the stone how he was looking for the giant who had captured the three princesses and asked the stone if it knew where the giant lived.

'I have been lying here at the bottom of this well for a thousand years but I have not yet heard where the giant has his castle. I do know

where he has his garden, though. It is at the bottom of another deep well. A wonderfully sweet smell will lead you to it. Now, I can tell you no more for I am a magic stone and can only speak once in a thousand years.'

Johnnie thanked the stone, climbed back out of the well with his bucket and once more travelled on from well to well. At last he reached one whose lovely smell spread far around. He let himself down to the bottom and, wonder of wonders, before him stretched a beautiful garden of flowers. In the middle of one plot were three mignonettes. These were the flowers which gave off the delicious fragrance. Johnnie bent to smell one of them and the flower suddenly spoke.

'Welcome, Johnnie, to the giant's magic garden. We are magic flowers that bloom only once in a hundred years. We will fulfil one wish for whoever stoops to smell us. Tell us what you want.'

Johnnie picked the flowers and asked the first to carry him unseen to the giant's castle.

'That is easy,' said the mignonette. 'The palace is at the bottom of the deepest well in the world. You would never get there on your own but with my help, we shall be there in a second.'

Before Johnnie could take stock of what was happening, he was standing in a huge golden hall. Here the three captive princesses had been put to work, sweeping with iron brooms — the one with a big nose, the second with big ears and the third all freckled. They recognized Johnnie at once and put their arms around him, kissing him until he blushed crimson. Then he felt the ground beneath his feet tremble. The giant was coming! Quickly Johnnie smelled the second flower and wished to be carried out of the well along with the princesses. In a trice, they were standing back above ground. The young man did not wait around for anything. He put two of the princesses on the hump on his back and the third, the one he liked best, he sat nicely on the hump at the front. Then he raced home as if his heels were on fire.

The giant also wasted no time. When he saw what had happened, he jumped straight into his seven-league boots and was off over hill and dale after the fugitives until the rivers almost broke their banks beneath his tread. He soon had them in sight and was ready to reach out his huge hand. Johnnie then remembered the third flower. He smelled it and begged the magic flower to change him at once into a miller and the three princesses into an old mill stone. His wish was hardly spoken when it was fulfilled.

The giant bent down to him and bellowed, 'Hey, miller, did you see three princesses around here? One has a big nose, the second big ears and the third is all freckled.'

'Of course I did,' the courageous Johnnie replied. 'Don't you see that old mill stone lying there? They hid under it like mice.'

The stupid giant lifted up the stone and eased his head under it. Straight away, Johnnie jumped high into the air and came straight back down on to the millstone. He thought the stone would smash the giant's head, but no such luck! The giant just sighed, 'What's that. It felt as if a pine cone fell on my head.'

Johnnie had now run out of ideas. Luckily, just then a dog raced by after a cat. 'Wait for me, don't run away,' it barked, but the cat had more sense. A run and a jump and she was on Johnnie's head. The dog did not hesitate, jumped and caught Johnnie's trousers.

'What's that?' thought the giant. 'My hat seems a bit tight today,' and he went on searching under the stone as though nothing had happened.

No doubt Johnnie would have been in trouble if it weren't for the fact that in the chace, the dog had shaken a little flea from his fur. 'Wait for me, don't run away!' cried the flea and she jumped on to the dog's tail.

The weight was now too much for the giant's head and it cracked like a hazel nut, much to Johnnie's relief. In a moment the millstone changed back again into the princesses. By some kind of magic they had changed. Not one of them was big-nosed, big-eared or all freckled any more. They were really beautiful now and

they heartily thanked Johnnie for everything he had done. What about Johnnie Hunchback, you ask? Believe it or not, his humps had disappeared. So they all joined hands and went to the royal palace. Of course, the king was beside himself with joy.

'Here you have the sceptre and the crown,' he told Johnnie, 'you may marry one of my daughters, if she will have you.' Now they were all so beautiful and all so even-tempered Johnnie found it impossible to choose between them. Just at that moment when Johnnie was trying to make his choice, up popped Mathilda, his true love, from the kitchen, to remind him that he had promised to marry her.

The princesses soon found husbands, and they all ruled the kingdom together, along with Johnnie and Mathilda, fairly and wisely for many years to come.

The Girl
with Blue Hair

'My dear Forget-Me-Not, why are you huddled so shyly in a corner? Come and tell us something nice,' the Rose Queen asked a young girl with sky blue eyes. This is the story the Forget-Me-Not told.

In a cottage at the foot of a hill there once lived a widow who gathered herbs for a living. She had just one son and his name was Jack. He was a strong young man, who was never afraid of work and gave a smile and a greeting to everyone he met. One day however, he seemed to lose his tongue. With each passing day he became more silent and more and more often would gaze longingly across the fields and forests and into the distance.

'Mother, it is high time I went out into the world to look for a wife. I am old enough now, and I want a companion. Besides, with three of us living here, it will lessen the work for all of us,' he told to his mother. The sensible woman agreed for she knew full well that all young things leave the nest when the time comes.

So Jack set out to find his bride. He went quite cheerfully and never looked back. He carried all his worldly wealth in a little bundle.

Sometimes it contained a poppyseed bun, other times a jam tart or even just a crust of dry bread – whatever good people chanced to give him along the way.

The day came when Jack reached a deep, black river. There was no bridge in sight and no ferry boat to be seen either. The young man sat down in the grass to decide what to do next. All around grew humble little blue flowers as though someone had spread a sky-blue carpet on the ground. It seemed to Jack that the flowers were still feeling the chill of morning, the way they huddled together in the grass. The boy felt sorry for them and leaned over one of them, trying to warm it a little with his own breath. At once the little blue flower opened wide and from its petals stepped a tiny girl. She had hair as blue as the sky above and a necklace of dewdrops around her neck. She was so lovely that Jack could not take his eyes off her. Every time he took a breath the girl grew a little until she was almost as tall as the wheat in the field.

'Who are you and what is your name?' Jack asked.

'I don't know,' said the girl sadly. 'One day we went swimming in the black river and since then I don't remember anything. That river is bewitched. Anyone who dips even a finger into it will never again remember anything. What is certain is that I have to look after these little blue flowers. Perhaps I am their sister. Perhaps it has always been so.'

'That is a sad affair,' said Jack, pitying the girl.

'Not at all.' said the girl 'I've got used to it. I would like to know what these flowers are called though. If something does not have a name it's as though it didn't exist.'

'You haven't got a name either,' Jack reminded the girl, 'and yet you exist.'

'Perhaps I do, perhaps I don't,' the girl laughed. 'I could be a dream for all you know.'

'Well, such dreams are to my liking,' said the boy and he quickly pinched his arm to see if he were dreaming. No, he wasn't, for it hurt!

'Do you know what?' asked Jack. 'I'll think up a name for you and for your little flowers. It will be something nice, to be sure, something blue-sounding.'

'I must have had a name at some time. The fairies from the other flowers told me that across the river, in a large garden, lives an old gnome. All the flowers that ever were in the world grow in that garden, and on each flower is written its name. No one dares to cross the spellbound river though, and even if they did, the gnome guards his flowers well,' the blue-haired girl sighed.

'If you will promise to marry me, I'll go across the black river into the gnome's garden. I'll read there what is written on the little blue flower.'

'All right,' the maiden agreed. 'I'll help you. Comb my hair and plait it.' Jack agreed and set to work. He plaited and plaited but the girl's hair was very long and it was quite a while before he had finished the task.

'Throw my plait over the river and use it to cross to the other bank,' the girl told him. 'Be careful you don't slip though! If you fall into the black river your memory will be gone forever!'

Jack did as the blue-haired girl said and started out across the blue plait to the mysterious garden.

'Forget me not,' the girl called after him.

'Forget me not,' Jack called to her.

Before long the young man reached the other bank safely.

There were thousands of flowers everywhere and all had their names written on them. 'Anemone, Harebell, Lily, Mignonette, Rosemary, Crocus, Speedwell, Houseleek, Gladiolus, and Hyacinth,' Jack read. There were so many names Jack could not count them all. In the end, he noticed a modest little blue flower in a corner, but before he could bend down to see its name, the old gnome, with his beard down to his waist and his eyes like burning coals appeared.

'Such impudence!' he shouted. 'If you dare to touch a single one of my flowers, I'll tear you to pieces on the spot.' With this, he changed into a fiery hound.

Jack was not afraid. Hurriedly, he plucked the little blue flower and raced over the blue plait across the river. The fiery hound was at his heels.

'My blue-haired girl, my love, save me!' called Jack. The girl on the other bank was startled. She jerked her head, the plait swung upwards and the unfortunate boy hurtled into the black river. It was a long time before the rapid stream carried him to the shore. Jack could not remember anything. He looked in puzzlement at the little blue flower and read its name with astonishment. Because it did not remind him of anything, he fastened it to his hat and went where his legs carried him. There was a strange sadness in his heart.

When the girl saw what had happened, she cried and called unhappily down the river, 'Forget me not! Forget me not!' but in vain. Time passed and the day came when the last of the blue flowers withered. The young girl had no one to care for any more and set out

downstream to seek her bridegroom. When she could bear her loneliness no longer, she asked some washerwomen to take her with them.

'What is your name?' they asked.

'I don't know,' the girl replied and the washerwomen chased her away.

'We can't make friends with someone who does not know her own name,' they thought.

The goose-girls would not accept her and neither would the reapers in the field. Not knowing where she was going, the girl wandered deep into the forest where she came to a little lake. It was a magical night and the moon glowed softly. Nymphs sprang from the water lilies and began to dance.

'Let me join you,' the blue-haired girl begged.

'Why not, flower fairy,' the nymphs replied. 'From this moment on, however, you must not say a single word or you will change forever into a flower.'

In despair, the girl promised and while she danced, the nymphs told her how they lured every person who came to them into the bottomless pool. There, the little green man, who was lord of the watery kingdom, turned them into fish. From that night, the blue-haired girl always danced with the nymphs under the light of the moon. She did not feel like singing even though a song might have relieved her sorrow. But not a single word passed her lips.

One evening when the moon was full, Jack's wanderings led him to that very place. He did not know how he had got there. He saw the dancing nymphs and the blue-haired girl among them, but he did not recognize her. She almost called out his name in joy and stopped herself only at the last moment. The nymphs ran up to Jack, however, circling him with light dancing steps and luring him to the bottomless pool. Jack could not resist and when the graceful beauties danced out on to the surface of the water, he hurried after them as though bewitched.

Now the blue-haired girl could not help herself and called anxiously, 'Stop, Jack, stop if you value your life!'

She had hardly spoken when the nymphs slipped back into the water lilies and the girl turned into a little blue flower, just like the one Jack carried on his hat. At that moment, Jack's memory returned.

'Now I know what your name is, my blue-haired love,' he sighed and bent down to the little flower to warm it with his breath. 'You are my Forget-Me-Not, that is your name,' he whispered. This time the flower did not open under his breath and no little blue-eyed fairy came out of it the way it had on the bank of the black river.

A soft voice came from the flower and spoke to Jack.

'Forget-Me-Not,' it begged.

'I shall never forget you,' Jack promised, and he picked the blue flower, fastened it close to his heart and returned to his cottage. As long as he lived, he did not seek another bride and was faithful till death to his blue-eyed love.

Aji Saka and the Magic Turban

'My name is Jasmine,' said a young prince, stepping up to take his turn at storytelling. 'My homeland is far away in the East and so I want to tell you a story which was whispered to me by the East Wind. Listen.'

Long, long ago, in a land far, far away, lived a wise man named Aji Saka. One day he decided to retire to a lonely cottage in the forest to meditate in peace and quiet about the secret of life. For seven days and seven nights Aji Saka sat in the middle of the jungle without moving. He did not eat and he did not drink. He just silently listened to the mysterious voices of the sky and the earth. His soul became filled with peace and a magical power entered his heart. It was a power capable of opening the flowers of the forest. Aji Saka had become a magician.

When he returned from his solitary time, back into the world of people, he called his servents Sembada and Doro and said to them, 'While I waited alone in the forest for magic power to find its way into my hands, the East Wind blew the scent of jasmine to me and with it, a very strange dream. I dreamed of a lovely island in crystal clear sea. The people there were poor and uneducated and they were ruled by a terrible cannibal king called Sang Prabu. I heard an unknown voice calling to me for help. So, my loyal servants, I want you to set out with me on a long journey.'

Sembada and Doro readily agreed but they wanted their master and teacher to tell them how they would get over the sea to the kingdom of the terrible cannibal king. Aji Saka smiled. 'The scent of jasmine spoke to me, so let jasmine decide,' he said.

With these words the wise man plucked a jasmine flower, dropped it to the ground and

held his magic hand over it. The flower opened and all at once it began to grow, and it grew and grew until it was so big, that all three of them could sit in it comfortably. Then it lifted them up to the skies like a flying carpet. They flew for a long time over land and sea and Aji Saka's white beard streamed behind them like a soft veil of mist. Then one day, the beard caught against the mountains of a mysterious island.

'We have arrived,' said Aji Saka and the jasmine flower drifted down with them to the shores of a bottomless mountain lake. 'You must now keep your eyes open, my friends,' the old man warned his servants. 'We are in the kingdom of spectres and demons who guard the way to the evil king, Sang Prabu. Sembada and I will set out on a journey inland while you, my faithful Doro, will remain here in the mountains where you must stop the demons helping their terrible cannibal king – take my magic dagger which will help you prevail over the mountain monsters. You must remember, however, that the monsters are able to change their appearance and can take on the likeness of your friends. Therefore, do not return the dagger to anyone but me for the only one they are unable to impersonate is myself.'

Doro promised to obey his master's commands and Aji Saka and the loyal Sembada climbed down the mountain into Mendang, the land of the powerful cannibal. They did not meet a living soul on the way. Indeed, it was as though the whole kingdom was under a spell. Only after a long time did they notice a very old man who was sitting and weaving baskets from palm fronds.

'Old man,' said Aji Saka, 'what has happened to the people of Mendang? It is as deserted and empty here as a country under a spell.'

'You speak the truth, oh man in a turban with a snow-white beard. The land of Mendang is a spellbound kingdom. Every morning the regent must bring our ruler a handsome young man to eat. The mothers and fathers have been terrified every morning when the sun begins to rise in the sky. It has reached the point now where tomorrow morning, the regent must bring his own son for Sang Prabu to eat because everybody else has run away.'

'Please lead me to the regent,' Aji Saka asked the old man, who agreed after much hesitation.

'Most noble regent and executor of the will of the powerful Sang Prabu,' Aji Saka exalted, bowing deeply to the desolate man seated on the throne. 'I am Aji Saka, teacher of the people, a wise man and a magician. I have heard of the misfortune which has afflicted your country. When the sun rises in the sky after the night, give me to your king to eat. You will see that I'll rid your kingdom of the cruel cannibal.'

'Your body is shrivelled and your hair is white,' answered the unhappy regent. 'Sang Prabu will refuse to eat an old man.'

Aji Saka just smiled, touched his head and in

a moment a handsome young man stood before the regent. Only the long white beard remained on his face. The regent was astonished.

'I see that your power is immense, venerable scholar. If you succeed in ridding our country of the terrible tyrant, I will fulfil your every wish.'

'My wishes are modest, oh regent!' Aji Saka replied. 'I want nothing more than enough land to go under my turban.'

'It would seem that your are an odd character, but I will fulfil your wish. For this, I give you my solemn promise,' the regent said. So the very next day, when the sun rose from the morning mists into the sky, the regent led Aji Saka before the throne of the terrible cannibal, the king Sang Prabu.

Sang Prabu was delighted when he saw the handsome white-bearded young man. He bared his teeth and his mouth watered. He stretched out his arm, seized the young man by his beard and pulled him towards the throne.

'What are your whiskers made of, my boy? Are they edible?' he growled.

'Just taste them, my lord,' Aji Saka laughed. 'You have never in your life eaten anything better.'

King Sang Prabu greedily pushed the beard into his mouth and began to swallow but the more he swallowed, the more beard there seemed to be until it filled the whole of his body. Inside the cannibal's body the beard changed into a fire and it burned the cruel king to ashes.

The whole country was thrilled when the news of the evil ruler's death spread. The regent summoned Aji Saka to his throne and thanked him with tears in his eyes. 'You asked for a small reward, noble Aji Saka,' he said. 'I will meet your wishes easily and with a light heart. Take as much earth as will go under your turban. It will belong to you for all eternity.'

With a smile, Aji Saka asked his servant Sembada to unwind the cloth bound round his head, but however hard the industrious Sembada tried, there was no end to the cloth of the turban. Before long, it covered the jungles and the mountains, the rivers and the lakes until the whole kingdom of Mendang lay beneath it. Thus Aji Saka become the lord and king of the country. He ruled wisely and kindly.

One day, he remembered his companion Doro. So he called his loyal Sembada and said to him. 'Go and find our friend Doro and tell him to found a large city at the foot of the mountains. It will guard the way to our kingdom. Bring also the magic dagger which is the emblem of my nobility and power.'

Sembada set out at once on his journey. After travelling for a long time he found Doro almost dead with exhaustion from his long struggle and asked Doro to hand over Aji Saka's magic dagger, but Doro refused.

'Your face looks like that of my loyal friend Sembada,' he said. 'However, Aji Saka warned me against apparitions which are able to take on themselves the likeness of all people. I must hand the magic dagger to Aji Saka alone. That is the promise I have made.'

'I, too, cannot go against my word,' Sembada replied. 'I will not go back without Aji Saka's dagger. I am bound to do so by my promise.'

So the two inseparable friends started a life and death struggle in order to fulfil the tasks set to each of them by their beloved teacher Aji Saka. They fought long and without mercy until both fell dead to the ground. They died in each other's arms.

When Sembada did not return for a long time, Aji Saka set out after him. At the foot of the mountain of spectres he found the dead bodies of his servants. He then remembered the order he had given to Doro and the task he had entrusted to Sembada. He understood that they had paid for their loyalty with their lives. With tears in his eyes, he picked up the magic dagger from the ground and in lasting memory of his dear servants, he used it to engrave in the rock this inscription:

'Ha na ca ra ka   – 'Loyal servants
da ta sa wa la   – fought together
pa da ja ya nya – both having equal
                        strength
ma ga ba ta nga' – until they became
                        lifeless bodies'

Just as he was cutting the last letter in the stone, a miracle happened! Doro and Sembada woke up from the sleep of death and fell at Aji Saka's feet in thanks.

'I also thank you for your loyalty,' said the wise Aji Saka, 'may this miraculous inscription in memory of your noble souls remain here for all the people of the land to see!'

And so it was.

When the East Wind sometimes blows the scent of jasmine to you and speaks the mysterious words 'ha na ca ra ka', remember that, far away from you, on a beautiful island called Java, little boys and girls are saying their alphabet in school.

Little Spinner

Prince Tulip never gave anyone any peace. He never stopped teasing the dancers, untying bows and pulling their plaits. 'You are a little rascal,' the Rose Queen chided. 'It would be better if you told us a nice story.'

Prince Tulip did as he was asked. This is his story.

A little spinner once appeared unexpectedly on the streets of a little town in Flanders. No one knew where she came from. Her skirt was nothing but patches, she had no shoes on her feet and the scarf on her head was so worn that it looked like a cobweb. Under her arm she carried an old spinning wheel.

'Take pity on me, please take in a poor orphan,' she cried as she went from house to house. 'I have not eaten for three days and I have nowhere to sleep.'

At every door she was turned away, for the country was very poor that year and no one had anything at all to spare. Then, in the end, good luck smiled on the destitute girl. She was taken in by a poor old woman who gave her a corner of her humble room to shelter in.

'Poor little thing,' said the good woman. 'For the present, make yourself a bed on that bench. You won't live in luxury with me, but no doubt we'll manage somehow together. Tell me, what do they call you?'

'I am called Spinner,' the girl answered, crying with happiness. When she had finished crying, she sat down in the corner with her spinning wheel and started to spin some flax she had brought with her. Then, when the girl had finished, the old woman took all that she spun to the market and sold it to the weavers.

One day the old woman brought home three lovely tulips instead of money and said with a sigh, 'My dear child, we'll have to make the best of it. The weavers have done no business today and have no money to pay with. Here you are, a piece of cheese at least.'

The girl smiled, thanked her and put the

cheese on a dish. 'It's all right, granny. Anyway, these tulips you brought me are so beautiful they will cheer me up!' she said, unable to tear herself away from the blooms.

'They look like three pretty girls,' she thought. 'It's a pity that my parents did not leave me three such little sisters in the world. I should love them so much.' For a moment, the little spinner grew sad and tears fell from her eyes into the flowers. Then, with a sigh, she sat down again to her work. She worked and worked, spinning her flax. The old woman also busied herself about the place.

The day passed swiftly. Before the little spinner knew it, it had begun to get dark. Tired out from her day's work, she began to doze a little over the spinning wheel. In her sleep, it seemed to her that she could hear soft footsteps. Patter, patter went the steps and little voices could be heard around her. The little spinner jumped and was startled, she opened her eyes. To her surprise, the balls of yarn were strewn all over the floor, in an untidy, tangled muddle. The cheese on the dish had been nibbled, too.

'Drat those mice!' the little Spinner wailed. 'Now I'll have to start my work all over again,' and, like it or not, she had no choice, but to sit down at the spinning wheel and set to work once more. All night she worked, and close to morning she began to feel tired once more. Unable to help it, she closed her tired eyes and rested her head on her spinning wheel. In her sleep, it seemed she could hear little footsteps on the floor and quiet laughter coming from all around the room. With great effort, the little Spinner made herself wake up. Once again, the balls of yarn had become tangled and now there was only a very small piece of cheese left!

'Oh what a useless wretch I am!' the girl sobbed. 'Whatever have I done to those cheeky mice that they should cause me so much trouble?' She ran to wake the good old woman to pour out her heart to her.

'Don't cry, little Spinner, don't be upset,' said the old woman kindly. 'We managed before and we'll manage again. It's a pity that we have no tomcat. He would know what to do with the mice. Don't worry. We'll get the better of them somehow.'

The old woman went straight away to the attic to get an old wire mousetrap. Together

they set it with the last of the cheese. Then they both went about their work. The old woman went off to market with the tangled balls of yarn, and the Spinner went off to her spinning wheel once more. When she had finally finished her spinning, her eyes began to close again in welcome sleep. Patter, patter she heard in her dreams. Little voices came from all sides. Suddenly, they stopped. Then she heard a sorrowful wail. Spinner awoke with a start. She could not believe her own eyes, for all the balls had once more been scattered about the place in a tangled mess and behold, there were three tiny girls huddled together in the mousetrap. They were so small that even if they were to stand on tiptoe, they would not see over your little finger. One had a red skirt, the second a blue skirt and the third a white one. They were all crying.

'Dear me, where have you came from?' Spinner cried.

'We are the sisters you wanted, born of your teardrops. We live in the tulips, the old woman brought home. Please let us out of this trap,' the little girls whimpered.

Spinner frowned. 'You call yourselves sisters!' she said sharply. 'Aren't you ashamed of spoiling my work, and nibbling the cheese that didn't belong to you. You made fun of me behind my back as well?'

'Don't be cross, we were only playing. We took only a little taste of cheese. Please, we'll never do it again,' the little girls cried, all together. 'Do please let us out!'

They were so unhappy and begged so sweetly that Spinner burst out laughing, opened the trap and let the little girls out. They ran across the floor and jumped straight back in their tulips. After a little while, they peeped over the sides.

'Spinner, if you promise not to punish us for annoying you, we'll help you to spin.'

Spinner promised and the little girls jumped out of the tulips and came running across the floor, right up to the spinning wheel. Two of them see-sawed on the treadle and the third straightened and wound the yarn. Spinner was speechless with amazement. The yarn they produced was as thin and delicate as a cobweb and sparkled like gold. In fact, it was gold! When the old woman returned from the market, she stood open-mouthed in wonder. There was Spinner, sitting in a corner of the floor and in the other corners were three little girls,

laughing and rolling the golden balls of yarn across the floor. Happiness reigned in their humble dwelling. Every day the old woman took the balls of gold yarn to the royal city and set up her stall right under the windows of the king's palace. Intrigued, the king ordered his courtiers to buy up all the yarn.

'Who is spinning such beautiful gold yarn?' he asked the old woman.

'Who else but Spinner, my dear foster child,' she replied.

The king couldn't sleep for curiosity. One day he called from his window, 'Tell your spinner that I am coming to visit her tomorrow.'

When the old woman heard this, she hurried straight home to tell her foster child the news. The three little Tulip girls put their heads together and whispered. Then they ran to the spinning wheel and set to work. When they had spun, they started to weave. When they had woven, they started to sew. When they had sown, they dressed Spinner in a splendid dress made of pure gold and covered in pearls and diamonds. 'Those are the tears you shed when you were all alone in the world,' they told little Spinner.

In the morning, when the king arrived at their home in his golden coach, he was met by a princess who was so beautiful that no one would have recognized her as the poor spinner

girl. The king fell in love with her at first sight. He took her, the old woman and the little girls to the royal castle and before long Spinner and the king were married. Their wedding is still spoken of to this day. Everyone ate, drank and made merry while the three tiny girls danced on the hand of the bride.

Before long, the royal couple had three delightful daughters. When they woke up crying at night as babies sometimes do, a patter, patter, patter could he heard in the room and tiny voices singing a tiny lullaby. After the babies were born, no one ever again saw the three little girls from the tulips. Spinner kept the tulips for the rest of her life, and by some strange magic they did not die. In fact they are blooming more beautifully than ever.

The Chrysanthemum

'The land of my birth is a magical eastern country which its people call the Heavenly Kingdom,' said the elegant and cool beauty, Chrysanthemum. 'In an ancient temple in the city of Cheng, there stands the statue of a young girl who, once, a long time ago, on the ninth day of the ninth month, drank wine from a goblet in which my magic flower floated. She became immortal, and since then, the people of that country look upon her as my protector. Today, though, I will tell you a story from the Country of the Rising Sun, which is my second homeland. They call me Ancient Mother of Kings, for I am the sign of the sun in that country. Now, my sisters, be silent and listen.'

Long, long ago, near a lake blanketed by water lilies, lived a lovely girl named Chrysanthemum. She was so beautiful that people compared her to the shining moon, and there was not one young man who dared to look her in the eye, perhaps because they thought it would spoil her beauty. Chrysanthemum loved to be alone. She would spend every moment she could walking in the flower garden.

One day, when she was resting after a full day's work on the bank of the lake, a handsome young man passed by. He walked with his head bowed, lost in thought. Suddenly, he caught a glimpse of Chrysanthemum's face reflected in the waters of the lake. The young man stopped

and turning around, found himself looking straight into Chrysanthemum's eyes. At that moment, love was born in their hearts.

'I love you,' he said.

'I love you,' she said.

They took each other by the hand and sat together on the soft grass. After a long time, the young man spoke. 'Thank you, my love, I am happy with you,' he said quietly.

Then, tears filled Chrysanthemum's eyes. 'How much happiness will we have? How long will you love me,' she sobbed. 'I want to know our future.'

The young man tried to comfort her and make light of it. Just then some big white birds flew above their heads and the boy called to them. 'Brother birds, please tell us how long our happiness will last!'

A little white feather with an answer written on it floated to the ground. 'You will have as many years of happiness as there are petals on the flower which the beautiful Chrysanthemum will choose.'

The young man and the girl ran eagerly to the garden. Chrysanthemum ran from flower to flower, but none of them seemed to have enough petals. At last her gaze fell on a wild marguerite. 'Count its petals. It seems to have the most of all,' she said to the young man. He quickly counted the snow white petals. Three times the young man counted, and three times the answer was the same. Finally he raised his head. There was sadness in his eyes.

'You have not chosen well, my beautiful Chrysanthemum,' he sighed. 'The petals of the marguerite do not amount to much in terms of a long life. Not many happy years are destined to us.'

Chrysanthemum burst into tears. All at once, a smile crossed her lips. Swiftly, she pulled the ornamental pin from her hair and used it to shred the petals of the marguerite into an almost endless number of very thin petals.

'Count them again,' she said to her love, but however many times he counted, the young man could find no end to them.

'We shall be happy together for ever,' Chrysanthemum cried with laughter and bent down to kiss the flower.

'My lovely, magical flower,' she said, 'I have nothing to reward with. The only thing I have to give you is my name.' That is how the Chrysanthemum was born.

'What about the little Chrysanthemum girl and her handsome young man? Did they have a long and happy life together?' the Rose Queen asked.

'Don't ask me, your majesty, ask the wild white birds,' Chrysanthemum replied with a smile.

Fairies

'Tell me, sister Lily, how many legends are woven around you?' the Rose Queen asked.

'As many as there are stars in the heavens,' answered the lovely princess. My story today is a simple one.'

There was once a young gardener. He had a heart of gold – he never upset anyone and if there were someone he could not help, at least they had his sympathy. As it goes in the world however, it is not always a bed of roses for good people. The young gardener was not getting on very well either. He lived from hand to mouth and on top of that, had a quarrelsome wife. She was forever scowling and grumbling until she had become quite ugly from her bad temper. The gardener was often sad at heart, but the thing that upset him most was the fact that they had no children. He thought that love for a child would soften his wife's nature.

One day, while tidying the attic, he found an old cracked mirror. He was pleased with his find. He wiped the cobwebs off it and took it downstairs.

'You fool,' his wife shouted. 'What good is such rubbish to us? You can go to the devil with it!'

Just then the mirror lit up as though with the light of candles and spoke to the gardener's wife. 'Don't be too hasty, woman!' it said. 'I have the power to fulfil everyone's most secret wish. Whichever one of you brings me the most beautiful flower will have a wish fulfilled. For one year and a day, he or she will enjoy untold happiness. After one year and a day however, that person will die.'

The gardener answered politely, 'A thousand thanks, magic mirror, but there is nothing we need. Life is dearer to us than all treasures of the world.'

With that his wife jumped in, 'Oh, you ungrateful good-for-nothing. Is that all I get for my love and care? If you want for nothing, then at least think of me. If you have one ounce of respect in your body, then you'll go with me to the garden to choose the most beautiful of the flowers for the mirror.'

The harassed gardener did not dare object. He went out of the house and picked a snow-white lily in the garden. 'All the flowers are lovely but none of them is as delicate and innocent as you, my dear lily. Perhaps the mirror will like you,' he thought.

His vengeful wife was watching him and when she saw that he really had selected the most beautiful of the flowers, she quickly plucked an ugly stinging nettle which grew on the grass. 'I should be stupid to sacrifice all my love for a single wish,' she said, smiling to herself. 'I'll force that nitwit to wish for the same as I do.'

When they returned to the house, they placed their gifts in front of the mirror.

'You have chosen well, gardener,' said the mirror. 'I like your flower. Tell me your most secret wish.'

Before the gardener could speak, his wife cried out, 'I want gold, pearls and precious jewels. I want to be rich and happy for the rest of my life!'

brought the most beautiful flower and I can read his most secret dream in his kind eyes. Gaze into me, good man.'

The gardener obeyed and he gasped. In the mirror he saw the face of a little girl as lovely and innocent as the flower of the white lily.

'That is your child, the one you have longed for so much,' said the mirror. 'When you wake up in the morning, she will be sleeping in a cot beside your bed.'

'And what about me?' shouted the quarrelsome woman. The mirror darkened once again.

'As you wish,' it said. 'I will reward you as well as you have deserved.' So when the impatient woman eagerly leaned towards the mirror, she saw in it the horrid face of a little girl with eyes which burned like nettle leaves. She angrily swiped at the mirror and with a single blow, smashed it into a thousand pieces.

Next morning, when the gardener and his wife awoke, they saw two cots standing at their bedside. In one was a little girl like a lily and in the other a horrid, grizzling child. The gardener was happy. He loved both the girls in the same way, he treated each one as though she were the apple of his eye and would not have harmed a hair of either girl's head. However, after a year and a day, in the middle of his greatest happiness, the good man died, as the mirror had promised. The gardener's wife now had to look after the children on her own.

As the years passed, Lily, for that is what her parents named her, became more beautiful and lovable. She was the image of her father. As for the other child, Nettie, she became as bad tempered and quarrelsome as her mother. In her mother's eyes, however, she could do no wrong. Both of them treated Lily as badly as they could, as often as they could. They thought up the hardest chores for her to do and forced

The modest man was just about to agree with her when the mirror grew dark with anger. 'You have no right to wish anything, you bad woman,' it said sharply to her. 'You husband her to sleep, winter and summer, on the porch. Lily often cried in a corner and often said prayers for her father whose face appeared to her in every mirror.

When the girls grew up, the widow began searching for a husband for Nettie. She dressed her in the most expensive clothes, decorated her with beautiful jewellery and made sure not a hair was out of place, while she daubed soot on Lily's face, and poured chaff into her hair, all to make sure suitors would not be distracted from her ugly sister. This was all in vain. The young men could not take their eyes off poor, tattered Lily, for her beauty shone through.

One day the ill-tempered widow took the heaviest jug and gave it to Lily, 'Go for water, you wretch!' she ordered. 'But not to the well behind the cottage. You'll go for it to the well in the dark forest. Perhaps the wolves there will tear you to pieces!'

Off went Lily, crying, for she was terrified. She had hardly begun to draw water from the forest well when an old beggarwoman appeared before her. 'Please give me a drink of water, young lady. I can't bend down for it myself,' she begged. Lily was glad to oblige, and when the old woman had drunk her fill, she again spoke to Lily.

'You have a kind heart, Lily,' said the old woman, who at once turned into a lovely forest nymph. 'Now go home and don't be afraid of anything. I will guard your way through the dark forest.'

Lily did not return to the cottage until late at night, hardly able to drag one foot after the other, she was so tired from her long walk. The widow shouted at her angrily and was nearly ready to pull her hair out by the roots.

'Don't be cross that I took so long,' Lily implored her. 'It is so far to the dark forest.'

The widow was thunderstruck. With every word, lovely white lilies fell from the girl's mouth and on the lilies sparkled dew drops made of real pearls and diamonds. When Lily told her what had happened at the well, the widow lost no time in sending the ugly Nettie into the dark forest.

'Take the very best jug and let the nymph drink as much as she likes,' she ordered.

Nettie went. She had barely begun to draw water from the well when a splendid princess in a rainbow dress stood beside her.

'Please give me a drink of water,' she begged. 'If I drew it myself, I might spoil my expensive clothes.'

'What do I care about your clothes, you proud show-off?' said Nettie, pushing her aside. 'Get out of my way. I am waiting for the good fairy who will reward me.' With these words, she flung the jugful of water over the princess's train. With that, the lovely princess changed into a forest nymph. 'Your heart is no different from your face,' said the nymph. 'Just go back home. You will get your reward.'

When, late in the night, Nettie returned to the cottage, her mother eagerly asked her, 'Do tell me, my dear daughter, how did you get on with the nymph?'

'Don't ask me to tell you!' her daughter snapped. 'I don't want to see another nymph as long as I live,' and as she spoke one toad after another jumped from her mouth. What a to-do that was! The widow was horrified even to look at her best-loved daughter, and on top of everything, the news of what had happened spread through the whole kingdom. Even the prince heard about it and rode up to see for himself. When the widow looked out of the window and saw the prince and his courtiers coming towards her house, she grabbed poor Lily and pushed her into a sack which she stood in a corner of the hall. She quickly dressed Nettie in her finest clothes and told her, 'Listen to what I say. You must not speak a single word in front of the prince.'

Nettie did as she was told, and when the prince came into the cottage, she threw loving glances in his direction and nodded her head like a donkey. The prince did not like the look of her at all.

'Why does your daughter not greet me in the manner befitting my royal person?' the prince demanded.

'Oh noble prince, she has been struck dumb by the sight of your handsome face,' the widow explained.

'Are you dumb?' said the prince, turning to Nettie.

'Yes, your highness,' the foolish girl replied and with every word a repulsive toad jumped from her mouth. The prince jumped back in disgust. Just then he heard a sigh coming from the sack in the corner.

'What have you got over there?' the prince demanded.

'What could I have there, my lord? Why nothing but a sack full of darkness!' she replied. The prince ignored her and quickly untied it. To his surprise, out peered a girl so lovely that he was overwhelmed by her beauty. Her eyes were filled with tears.

'Do they call you Darkness?' asked the prince in surprise.

'Oh no, your highness, my name is Lily,' the girl answered modestly and with every word a pure white, sparkling lily fell from her lips. The prince fell in love with Lily the moment he set eyes upon her and because Lily also liked him, she did not hesitate when he asked her to marry him.

There followed a wedding which is talked about to this day. Lily danced for seven days and nights with her husband and all that time with every word she spoke a lovely lily full of pearls and diamonds fell from her lips. There is now a lily in the royal coat of arms and kings tell their grandchildren the story of lovely Lily.

If you are wondering what happened to Nettie. They say that the stork king once flew to her cottage and because she had very bad luck finding a husband, she finally married him. Evil tongues claim that she caught her stork bridegroom rather on the toads than on her beauty. Who knows?

All that we can be certain of is that the stork kingdom is somewhere beyond the dark forest and its coat-of-arms is a toad in a stork's beak. That is the end of the story.

Father of the Flowers

A princess in a splendid scarlet skirt danced up to the Queen's throne, bowed deeply and said, 'Your majesty, my name is peony and my gift to you is a story from a kingdom far away in the East. Listen.'

During the rule of the noble Yin-Tsong, a man named Tsien-Sien lived in a certain village. From the time he was very young, his greatest love was flowers. He loved them as his own children, he dreamed about them and wrote beautiful songs about them. Around his simple cottage with its thatched roof was a lovely garden filled with delicious scents and brilliant colours. Not a single day went by that Tsien-Sien did not plant a new seed or the seedling of a new, rare flower. Each day he would rise at dawn to tend his beloved flowers, not stopping to rest until sunset. Sometimes even at night he would find himself drawn to their fragrance and beauty. There was no more beautiful garden in the whole country.

People began calling Tsien-Sien The Father of Flowers. He loved to show spellbound visitors his magic kingdom but no one was allowed to pick a single flower.

'I do not want to see my flowers cry,' he would say, 'for it would break my heart.'

One day a blind man wandered into Tsien-Sien's garden. He carried a basket full of wonderful peony plants the like of which Tsien-Sien had never seen before.

'What kind of peonies are these beauties?' he asked in wonder.

Touching each one gently in turn, the blind man said, 'This one is called the Golden Stairway, that one the Green Butterfly. This one is the Wealth of the Water Melon.' 'Ah,' he said, breathing the fragrance of another, 'these two I like best of all. They are called the Glittering Blue Lion and the Head of the Great Red Lion. How do you like them?'

Tsien-Sien praised the great beauty of the flowers but inside, trembled with worry lest the blind man should go off again with his treasure. The Father of Flowers so wished to have these flowers blooming in his garden!

'How much do you want for these flowers?' Tsien-Sien cried longingly.

The old man laughed. 'They are too expensive even for the king,' the blind man replied, but when Tsien-Sien sighed in disappointment, the blind man said, 'I will leave them for you if you will give me your greatest treasure of all – your eyes.'

Tsien-Sien agreed, and with that, the old man gently touched his eyelids. All at once, Tsien-Sien found himself surrounded by impenetrable darkness, for he was, indeed, now blind. He heard the old man going away but the scent of his peonies remained. Reaching out, Tsien-Sien felt the basket of flowers and planted them by touch in the best plot in his garden. He was happy. Word of the peonies' beauty soon spread throughout the region. People came from all parts of the land to admire their splendour. They started to call Tsien-Sien The Man who gave His Eyes to the Flowers.

From then on Tsien-Sien spent all his time near his beloved peonies. He cared for them with unfailing devotion and every morning he made an offering to the spirit of the flowers. Eternal spring came to the garden, but his happiness did not last long. In a nearby town

lived Tchang-Oey, the son of a mandarin. He was a cruel young man who spent every night with his wild friends, going from tavern to tavern causing all manner of grief and sorrow wherever they went.

One morning, after a long night of revelry Tchang-Oey was on his way home with his gang. The road took him near Tsien-Sien's garden. The peonies were then in full bloom and Tchang-Oey froze on the spot.

'The king himself does not have such magnificent flowers in his garden,' he cried and ran to see them.

Tsien-Sien, afraid of what might happen, barred the way, crying, 'Whoever harms the flowers will harm the gods. What is it you want in my garden?'

Tchang-Oey stood still for a moment, but then he shouted haughtily, 'Do you not know me, old man? That alone would be enough for me to punish you. I am the noble Tchang-Oey, son of a mandarin, whose voice should be recognized even by blind man. Get out of my way, I am going to pick your flowers.'

Tsien-Sien fell at Tchang-Oey's feet and begged that his beloved flowers be spared. Tchang-Oey, still full of wine from his night of carousing kicked the old man out of his way and ordered his companions to cut down the peonies with their swords. In so doing, they covered the garden with a carpet of fragrant

flowers. Then he ordered them to open a flagon of wine and in a wild bout of drinking, Tchang-Oey did nothing but make fun of Tsien-Sien's blindness. When the cruel louts had at last gone away, Tsien-Sien crept through his garden and with trembling hands, felt for the fallen flowers. His arms full of broken blossoms, he sat beneath the trees and cried bitter tears. For a long time he cried, and when the final tear had fallen from his sightless eyes, Tsien-Sien was amazed. The whole world suddenly glowed with rainbow colours and Tsien-Sien realized that he could see again.

Enchanted, he looked once more upon his flowering garden and was surprised to find all the peony blooms again in place, even more colourful than before. Just then, a lovely girl appeared before him. Tsien-Sien guessed it was this girl who had caused his beloved flowers to be restored and also returned his lost sight.

'What is your name, enchanted being?' he whispered with reverence.

'I must not tell you my name,' the girl replied, 'but this I can say. I am the spirit of the flowers and I serve the powerful Queen of Gardens, Tchy-Wan-Man. My mistress heard about your love for flowers and she sent me here help you. From today, you will be under her protection.'

With these words, the girl disappeared and the happy Tsien-Sien set out to wander through his kingdom once more able to rejoice in its wonderful sights. Word of the miracle in Tsien-Sien's garden reached every ear and crowds of inquisitive people came to witness the sight of the magic peonies. When Tchang-Oey heard about it, an idea was born in his vengeful heart. He went straight away to the governor of the province.

'Tsien-Sien is a wizard,' he lied. 'He has made the acquaintance of evil forces and with the help of their magic he intends harming innocent people. I want him to be thrown into prison.'

So what Tchang-Oey wanted happened. The unfortunate Tsien-Sien was arrested by the guards and shut up in an underground cell. The following day he was to be put to death. Just as the prison gate closed behind him however, he heard once more the musical voice of the flower spirit.

'Do not be afraid, Tsien-Sien, Father of the Flowers,' she said. 'The Queen of Gardens will fulfil her promise. Before one day has passed, you will be free and the evil Tchang-Oey will not escape punishment.' The old man trusted the voice and slept peacefully that night.

Meanwhile, Tchang-Oey was immensely pleased with his shameful deed and so as to satisfy his thirst for revenge even more, he went once again to Tsien-Sien's garden. When he got to the gate, he froze in amazement. All the flowers lay withered on the ground as though cast aside by a merciless hand.

'I was right,' Tchang-Oey cried. 'The old man is ruled by witches' powers. From his prison he has used spells and magic to destroy all the flowers so that we could not enjoy their beauty.'

Suddenly a hurricane arose and whirlwinds began to chase all over the garden, then changed into young girls with flowing hair. 'We are sisters who live in this garden,' they cried, 'and we have come to get you, you evil, proud Tchang-Oey! We shall get back at you for what you have done to our father Tsien-Sien. We shall dance you to death.'

Before Tchang-Oey could come to his senses, they had grasped him round the waist and bore him away in a wild dance on the wind. Around and around, the sisters whirled him, never ceasing in their fandango, until at last, exhausted, Tchan-Oey collapsed and died.

When the governor heard of the young thug's death, he became frightened and with many humble apologies, set Tsien-Sien free. The happy old man was at last able to return to his beloved flowers. While he walked in his garden, enjoying their splendid shapes and colours, a gentle breeze began to blow. Music sounded and a glowing cloud appeared on the horizon. An intoxicatingly beautiful fragrance spread throughout the garden and blue phoenixes and snow-white storks flew in the sky. From the cloud stepped a goddess. Tsien-Sien bowed low and the goddess spoke in a ringing voice, 'Tsien-Sien, Father of the Flowers, you have done enough good deeds. The Lord of the Heavens wishes to reward your love of flowers and asks you to join him in his heavenly home.'

Tsien-Sien once more bowed as a sign of gratitude and then, at a gesture from the goddess, he stepped on to the cloud. Together with his cottage, the flowers and trees and all he had loved, it rose slowly up to the heavens. The people of the village waved to Tsien-Sien, smiling happily. From that day the village changed its name. It is now called Ching-Sien-Li, or the village of the immortal who rose to the heavens. It is also called the Village of a Hundred Flowers.

Who was Drowned?

'I will tell you a story about Gotham,' said the fragrant Sweet Pea, who was an elegant young man. 'The people of Gotham have always been known as the biggest fools under the sun, but each of them behaves as though he had swallowed all the wisdom of the world.'

'Tell us your story,' the Rose Queen commanded and the Sweet Pea began.

Once upon a time, so the story goes, the Mayor of Gotham arose one morning with the desire to have a handsome carp from the local pond. He did not feel like going fishing on his own, so he summoned his first counsellor, then his second counsellor, the night watchman and the constable on the beat. He gave each of them a fishing rod, a dip net and landing net and they were ready to be off when something suddenly occurred to him.

'I say, what if one of us should drown while fishing? There are so many of us that we might not even notice it. It would be better for us to count ourselves first. I say, clerk, get to work – but, I'm telling you, make a proper job of it,' he commanded.

From sheer self-importance, the clerk grew a fraction taller. He stood the mayor and all the other anglers properly in a line and, to make doubly sure, he pointed a finger at each one while carefully checking them off on his other hand. He also counted out loud. 'One, two, three, four, five. There are five of you, Mr Mayor!' he said. Indeed, as proof, he raised his hand with his fingers spread triumphantly, but the mayor was a prudent fellow, for how else could he be mayor of such a famous town? 'Do you truly have all five fingers on your hand?' he asked. 'You'd better count and check,' said the mayor.

The clerk hurried as much as he could without making a mistake in his sums. 'Cross my heart, there are five,' he announced shortly.

'Are you absolutely sure?' the mayor asked.

'Almost,' the clerk muttered, but when he saw that the mayor looked cross, an idea came into his head. 'I've got it, I've got it! I shall pick five sweet peas from the flower bed and fasten one on to each of your hats. If none are left over, you can bet whatever you like that there really are five of you.'

In a trice, he had done as he said he would. There were neither too few or too many flowers.

'This idea of yours will only work if we're all wearing hats,' the mayor said. 'I say, take your hats off everyone.' They all took their hats off and the clerk counted first the heads and then the hats. 'No heads and no hats are missing,' he informed them solemnly. 'There are five of you as sure as I am public clerk in Gotham.'

At last the mayor was content. They all set out in single file to go fishing.

The banks of the pond were slippery. The others were only just able to grab the night watchman at the last minute before he and his staff slithered into the water together.

'Are we all here?' the mayor asked anxiously. 'Perhaps we should count ourselves again in case, God forbid, one of us has drowned.'

He stood with the others in a straight row, as he had observed the clerk doing, and started counting with his forefinger but he forgot to point to himself. 'One, two, three, four…' he counted slowly, his knees knocking with horror.

'Lord-a-mercy, we're one too few,' he cried. 'Someone has drowned.'

The first counsellor was doubtful. He stepped out of line, put the mayor in his place and started counting with his forefinger, but he also forgot to point to himself. 'Great Scott! There really are only four of us,' he said in shock. 'It isn't possible for both of us to be mistaken. Oh dear, dear. Which one of us, poor wretch, has got himself drowned?' he wailed.

'Let him come forward himself,' the second counsellor proposed.

'You fool,' said the mayor disdainfully. 'I've got a better idea. Let us take our hats off and lay them on the grass. The one whose hat is missing will be the one who was drowned.'

So they did as the mayor said.

'Is there anyone without a hat?' the wise man asked.

No one was hatless. To make certain, the mayor counted the hats. There were five. To make certain, he also counted the sweet pea flowers. All there.

'God be praised, we are all here, no one has drowned. We probably counted wrongly before.' They all cheered.

'Just a minute,' said the mayor. 'Wouldn't it be a better idea to count our heads to find whether there is one without a hat.'

Once more, he put his companions in a line and started counting with his forefinger, this time forgetting to count his own head. 'One,

two, three, four… Oh no! One head is missing. One of us really has drowned!' he wailed. 'But whose is the hat that is left over?'

'Of course! It belongs to the drowned man,' the second counsellor decided. 'He probably left it on the bank. Poor chap, his head will be properly chilled.'

They all started crying over the poor chap's fate.

'Upon my soul, which one of us, in fact, has been drowned?' asked the constable.

'It wasn't me,' they all answered together. Not one of them knew what to do.

'I know!' said the mayor. 'We'll put our hats on again. The one whose hat is still on the grass is the one who has drowned.' All of them bent down obediently, picked their hats up and put them on. They were dumbfounded. There was no hat left lying on the grass.

'Well, that's the limit. It just beats me,' the mayor said, bewildered. 'Let me tell you, neighbours, a horrible misfortune has befallen us. We are bewitched.'

All of them could feel their hair stand on end and they all began to cry with fear.

Just then, a stranger on a black horse passed by. 'What is making you so unhappy, good people? Can I help in any way?' he asked.

Sobbing their hearts out, the five companions told the stranger their story. 'Please count us, stranger,' they begged him. 'Tell us whether one of us has been drowned.'

The stranger laughed and he counted them smartly with his whip on their backs. 'There are five of you, good people. No one is missing,' he announced.

'Are you sure?' asked the mayor, suspiciously.

'For all I care, I'll count you ten times if that's what you want,' the waggish fellow cried, and he laughed and laughed and he counted and counted until the people of Gotham had tears of pain rolling down their cheeks.

'That's enough! We believe you now,' the mayor cried. 'My goodness, you know how to count — like the crack of a whip. How can we pay you?'

The stranger was going to the neighbouring town to visit his love. 'I know! Give me those sweet pea flowers. They will make a nice posy for my girl.'

The Gotham folk were glad to oblige and they hurried home to cool their counted backs. 'Stupid fellow,' the mayor complained. 'He can count so well and yet he asked so little for it.'

So that is the end of the story, except for one thing. Since that time, it is said that the young men of Gotham take bunches of sweet peas when they go courting. Do you know how they count at the Town Hall? Why, with a whip across people's backs. It's really best not to visit Gotham at all, if you can help it!

The Devil and the Tinker

'Long, long ago, an enchantress whose name was Meda was in the middle of preparing a youth potion made from magic herbs. Several drops fell to the floor and from those drops grew a beautiful but poisonous flower. That is, they say, how I, the Autumn Crocus, came into the world,' thus spoke a good-looking young prince with a bell in his hair. 'Do not be afraid little flowers,' he said, 'I will not harm you. Anyway, that's not my story. I have quite a different tale to tell.'

There was once a young tinker wandering the world. He went cheerfully from village to village, calling loudly into every window, 'Here's the tinker, folks, please attend. Bring out your pots and jugs to mend.'

He had no shortage of work. There were plenty of old broken pots and cracked jugs in every cottage. The young man did not do too badly.

One day, on his journeying, he reached a little brook. Beyond the brook was a little meadow and in the meadow a cottage. All around the cottage, wherever the eye could see, the fragile bells of Autumn Crocuses were flowering in the autumn sun. Just then, a white

haired old woman, a herb gatherer, came out of the cottage.

'Thank goodness I saw you,' she called, 'I need you to mend a little pot for me.'

'No sooner said than done,' answered the young man cheerfully and set to work straight away. He was soon finished. The old woman was pleased but she looked troubled.

'How can I pay you?' she said in a worried voice. 'I am so poor, I haven't got so much as one penny.'

'What you have not got you cannot give,' the tinker said, dismissing her thanks. 'Anyway, I can manage without. The main thing is that I have made you happy.'

'That you did, my young friend,' the old lady agreed and dipped into her pocket. 'There is something I can give to you. Look!' She handed the young man a shrivelled walnut. 'Can you guess what is in it?'

'Nothing!' the tinker laughed.

'Oh but there is something there,' said the old lady. 'Have another guess.'

The young man racked his brains but he could think of nothing.

'Of course, there is darkness there,' said the herb gatherer and she laughed at the joke she had played on the young fellow. 'Take this nut with you on your travels, it might come in useful. Also, should a time come when you don't know what to do, come back to me and perhaps I'll be able to help you.'

The tinker thanked her and went his merry way. One day he reached a dark forest. A red flame suddenly shot up from the earth in front of him and from it sprang hundreds of little white flames. They all set off in a crowd to the forest.

'What are you doing? you'll start a fire,' the young man shouted at the flames and he tried to trample out the fire. In a moment the flames turned into white sheep and the red flame became a hairy devil. He had horns like an old ram. The devil blew sparks from his nose and stamped his hooves on the ground till it trembled.

'Whoever sees the devil grazing his sheep will go to hell,' he laughed. 'That is the law. Prepare for your journey, you wretch!'

It goes without saying that the tinker was not too keen on going to hell so he tried to talk the devil out of it.

'All right,' said the devil, 'because you're such a talkative fellow, perhaps you can talk your way out of this. We'll set each other riddles. If you win, I'll give you my sheep, but woe betide you if you lose, for then I'll take your soul.'

The tinker remembered the old woman and taking from his pocket the empty walnut he asked, 'You guess first, then, you scruffy old devil. What's in this nut?'

'That's a devilish problem,' said the devil scratching between his horns. 'Whatever could be there. A kernel? Not on your life! Nothing? Rubbish! I've got it, little tinker, there's darkness in there!'

This put the tinker in a fix. He was shaking with terror while the devil was laughing so much, his mouth was on fire.

'Get ready for the journey, you poor worm, I'll take you to hell!' he rejoiced.

The tinker suddenly got an idea. 'He who laughs last, laughs longest,' he replied. 'You said there was darkness in there, so show me!'

The devil took the nut and cracked it between his teeth. Of course, as soon as the nut was opened, the light came in and it was the devil's own job to prove it had ever been dark in there! The tinker jumped for joy.

'I've won,' he cried. 'Hand over your sheep, devil.'

The devil had no intention of giving up so easily, however, 'It's my turn now,' he growled. 'Before tomorrow morning you must find me a son who is older than his own father. If you fail, then it is hell for you. Let me tell you this, don't you try to hide from me! I'll find you wherever you go.' Saying this, he stamped his hoof on the ground and he and his herd disappeared.

The poor little tinker! In vain he tried to solve the devil's riddle. Could he possibly find a son older than his father? Could anyone know a father who would be younger than his son? In his moment of need, he remembered the old herb gatherer. He ran to her cottage, knocked on the gate, and told her of his misfortune.

'That's easy, little tinker,' said the old woman with a smile. 'Look out into the meadow. What do you see?'

'I don't see anything, granny, just flowering Autumn Crocuses.'

'That's it — Autumn Crocuses,' the herb gatherer said, nodding. 'The Autumn Crocus is the answer that you need. In the spring, it sends up a stem from the earth and on that stem is a fruit containing the seed. That fruit is the son. It is not until autumn that the father, the Autumn Crocus flower, appears in the meadow. Like that, the father is always younger than his own son. The opposite is the case with all other flowers and plants. First of all the flower blooms and only then does the fruit ripen. So you see, you have won.'

The tinker was overjoyed. He thanked the wise old lady from the bottom of his heart and the moment the first cock crowed in the village, he plucked an Autumn Crocus and went off to his meeting with the devil. The devil was already waiting for him. He was rubbing his clawed fists together and licking his lips with his fiery tongue.

'Did you find out?' he jeered at the young man.

'Yes, I did,' the tinker answered bravely and showed the devil the Autumn Crocus. 'Just listen! In the spring the crocus son emerges from the ground and only in the autumn does the flower come from the fruit. Here you have it. This is the father which came from the son.'

At that moment a bolt of lighting struck the ground before them, and where it struck a great gash opened up in the earth and swallowed up the devil.

The tinker gathered together his flock and drove them back to the old herb gatherer's cottage. 'I've wandered enough,' he thought, 'I'll build my own cottage not far from the herb gatherer and I'll graze my sheep in the meadow. He did as he said, even helping the old woman

once or twice when she was in trouble. Let it not be said in vain that the devil never sleeps. He could not reconcile himself to defeat and at a loss what to do otherwise, decided to poison all the young man's sheep. One day he crept secretly into the meadow where the sheep used to graze and spat poison into each Autumn Crocus flower. From that time, Autumn Crocuses have been poisonous.

'And that is the true story of how it is with us,' said the Autumn Crocus, ending his tale.

The Rose Queen frowned. 'And what about the sheep?' she asked. 'Were they poisoned?'

'Oh no, not at all,' the Autumn Crocus said airily. 'They were sheep from hell and so the devilish poison did not harm them. That, my friends, is truly the end of the tale,' he said, ringing his bell.

The Little Minstrel

The charming princess Aster spun around in her rainbow skirt and blew kisses to her partners before she started her story.

A very long time ago, the whole earth was governed by one king. His magic palace was guarded by golden dragons and as a sign of his great power, the sun shone, day and night on the highest tower. All the riches of the world belonged to him. He ruled over the sea and the land, over the rivers and the mountains. He governed wisely and justly and the people of the earth loved him. The king was very happy.

One day, however, the king's counsellors found their master in deep despair. He sat, head in hands, sighing. 'I have everything I could ever want. Riches, fame and the love of my people. And yet the seed of jealousy has taken root in my heart. Very far away from here, in the enchanted Midnight Garden, stands a tree that has grown right up to the heavens. In its crown stands the palace of my brother, the king of all the heavens. The stars flower in the branches of that tree. My most heartfelt wish is for my earth to flower like the shining night sky. I would like all of my subjects to be able to gather a bunch of stars to gladden their hearts. You must find in my kingdom a man strong enough to shake the stars from the heavenly tree, or I shall never be content.

The counsellors immediately sent messengers to all corners of the earth to tell the people of the king's wishes. Very soon, brave men from all over the kingdom travelled to the Midnight Garden to try to bring happiness to their king, but even when they put all their strength together, they couldn't do it.

One day a little travelling minstrel heard about the emperor's wish. He was a poor orphan with no family in the world. He went from house to house, singing his songs, to make a living. When he sang, people couldn't help but smile and dance. Then, he would take out his flute and play with such sensitivity that his audience could not hold back their tears. They would cry until the boy took the instrument from his lips.

When the boy heard of the king's sorrow, he went straight to the Midnight Garden, even though he was small and not very strong. He travelled day and night and when at last he arrived at the Midnight Garden, he sat under the heavenly tree and began to sing. He sang such merry little songs the tree began to shake with silent laughter, but not a single star fell from its branches. Then the boy took out his little flute and the tune he played reminded him of the days he spent with his mother, when he was still very small. He played so sweetly that the mighty tree shook with great heaving sobs from its roots to its crown. As the tree shook, glowing stars began to fall from its branches. Wherever they fell, beautiful flowers bloomed.

All the people looked on in astonishment. 'The stars are flowering,' they cried, and everyone who had loneliness or sorrow in his heart, picked a bunch of flowering stars for comfort. When the earthly king heard of this, his heart grew light and the sun shone ever brighter over his palace. The king then ordered that the young minstrel be brought to his palace. The king was so grateful to the minstrel he wanted to make him his son, but the minstrel was nowhere to be found. Perhaps he is still to be found wandering the earth reaching peoples' hearts with his music. And we, the stars, are still flowering all over the earth. We are called Asters.

The Scarecrow Knight

'Over hill and over dale, I come to you to bring my tale,' sang the joker, Love-lies-bleeding. He wore spikes of red flowers in his hat and smiling cheekily at the Rose Queen, whispered, 'Listen!'

Almost right at the end of the world, in a far off godforsaken place, in a tiny out-of-the-way village, there once lived a young wood-carver named Andrew. With his knife he could carve anything you could think of – a wooden bowl, a spoon or a boat from bark: a hare, a squirrel, a little dog, a cot with a doll in it, a drummerboy with his drum, a soldier on guard and even an elaborate carriage complete with a nobleman seated inside, and a footman on the step. All the village children would flock to Andrew's cottage, begging for all sorts of toys and Andrew, being a generous young man, never sent them away empty-handed. However, giving things

away without payment doesn't put food on the table, and so Andrew grew poorer day by day. So while the sons of rich farmers rode around on proud horses, their reins jangling with gold and bright with ribbons so that the village girls could hardly keep their eyes off them, Andrew stayed indoors, too ashamed to go out in case some scornful girl should shout after him, 'Hey rags and tatters, where's your pride? You must go to the devil to find a bride.'

'Just you wait. I'll bring home such a beautiful bride one day that all the other young men will envy me,' Andrew decided.

Then, one day, a strange sort of creature came knocking at Andrew's door. It was neither a woman, nor a man. Its hair was emerald green and on its head it wore a toadstool hat with a jay's feather stuck in it. It had the legs of a frog, the wings of a bird, and the eyes of an owl.

'My grandfather was a goblin, my father was a goblin and among all the goblins I am a hobgoblin,' the uninvited guest piped. 'If you will carve me a nice pair of clogs with my little knife, Andrew, I'll reward you well.'

Andrew did not need much persuading and got down to the job straight away. Very soon the clogs were shaped, but the carver had hardly finished when they sprang from his grasp and started to run off on their own. The goblin jumped right into them and was off.

Andrew sighed with relief, at least the little devil was gone. He had gone without paying though, and once more Andrew was without money for his work. The hobgoblin had forgotten to take his knife with him, however, and Andrew, pleased that he had gained some small reward for his labours, began to carve with it. He began to carve a little horse, and just as he was putting the finishing touches to its last hoof,

the little horse reared upon its hind legs and neighed,

'Saddle me without delay,

Andrew, let's be on our way,

We have before us quite a ride

For we are off to fetch your bride.'

Andrew, being a cheerful fellow at heart, laughed and said, 'And why not? But first I must dress myself properly for that journey. I'll dress myself up as a knight, to give the boys and girls in the village something to look at.' He set to work at once. Instead of armour, he pulled on an old barrel around his body, instead of a helmet, he put a cracked pot on his head, and for a lance he took a broom stick with a pair of old trousers tied to it for a pennant. He wielded the door to the goat pen as a shield. So he started his journey – and what a journey!

The horse was so small that Andrew's feet dragged along the ground until a cloud of dust bellowed out behind him. People from all over the village came running. They laughed and shouted out, 'Long live the good knight Scarecrow! Where are you going, your lordship? Would you be off to fetch your bride?'

Andrew greeted them solemnly and answered, 'Of course I am going for my bride. I shall bring back to my cottage the most beautiful princess living on earth.'

The villagers could have split their sides with mirth. They all followed him to the outskirts of the village and waved him off, still roaring with laughter. Andrew did not care at all. The horse's hooves went clip, clop, clip, clop, and Andrew sang to their rhythm. In this way, the journey passed quite pleasantly.

After a while, the carved wooden horse and its rider came to an old weeping willow. It could see itself in a pool and as it looked, tears flowed from its old knots. 'Oh dear, how ugly I am!' the tree wept. 'Please, Andrew, cut my hair with your magic knife so that I don't look so untidy!' Andrew was glad to oblige but just as he cut the last wand, the willow tree turned into a kindly old woman.

'Thank you, young man, I shall reward you for your kindness. Listen carefully! It will soon be Midsummer's Eve, and at this time some flowers gain a magical power. At midnight, you must pick a bunch of Love-lies-bleeding. If you place a flower in the right shoe of a sick girl, she will become well at once. If you place a flower in a girl's left slipper, she will fall in love with you at once and forever.'

Andrew thanked the old lady and followed her instructions. As soon as day broke, he set out on his journey once more. He did not know how long the journey took, but one day he arrived at a prosperous royal city. All this wealth did not seem to make the people happy, however, for they all went about with their heads bowed, and were not even amused at the ridiculous appearance of the newcomer. All the houses of the city were draped in black.

'The daughter of our noble king is dying,' an old stallholder told Andrew. He has promised his daughter and half of his kingdom to the one who will bring her back to health, but wise doctors and powerful magicians come to the palace day after day and the princess just gets worse.'

'I will do what I can for the princess,' thought Andrew and made his way to the palace. He rode on his little horse right into the throne room, where he found the king, sobbing in despair. The sick princess was huddled beside him on her throne. She was as pale and transparent as the flame of a candle.

'I have come to make your daughter well again, your highness Mr King, sir,' the un-likely healer announced. The king sighed despondently.

'Many have come with the same intention, young man. Each one of them has ended up in the hands of my executioner. If your life is dear to you, don't even attempt a cure, for I am a desperate man.'

Andrew was not deterred by this, however. He merely asked to be allowed into the princess's room for a moment when she was asleep at night. The king agreed and Andrew crept in. There he placed a Love-lies-bleeding flower in the princess's right shoe. When the sick princess put her shoes on the next morning,

her illness faded away and she immediately became well again. The king was overjoyed.

'My dear daughter, this is your bridegroom,' said the king to his daughter. 'He has saved your life and for that I have promised him your hand in marriage along with half the kingdom.'

The princess cast a disdainful glance at Andrew, gave a satiric laugh and then scowled, 'That Scarecrow Knight? I could just as well get married to the scarecrow in the field. Let him

first find my lost ring in the lake, then we'll see.'
The princess knew very well that the lake was
bottomless and Andrew soon found that out,
too. He sat sadly on the bank and racked his
brains for a solution. Then he heard the tapping
of clogs, and the hobgoblin ran past like the
wind.

'You fool, what do you think you have my
magic knife for?' he called as he went by. 'Carve
a wooden fish, you'll see that it will help you.'
Andrew at once got down to the job as the
hobgoblin had advised. Just as he was putting
the finishing touches to its last fin, the fish
wriggled and jumped into the lake. In a moment, it was back at the surface with the lost
ring in its mouth. As soon as the princess saw
her lost ring, she grew pale with anger.

'I want him to fetch my golden scarf before
morning. The wind carried it off high above the
clouds,' she said. Andrew knew what he should
do now, and lost no time in carving a little lark
out of wood. He was just putting the finishing

touches on its little feathers, when the lark
soared upwards to the heavens and in a moment
brought back the princess's scarf in its beak.
The princess was beside herself with rage.

'Don't rejoice yet, you Scarecrow Knight!
Before morning you must bring me seven
dragon heads. Then I will marry you. If you do
not fulfil the task, you will lose your head.'

Now Andrew was in a pretty pickle. What
could he possibly carve with the magic knife
which would be able to kill a seven-headed
dragon? Just then he heard the tap of clogs.

'Give me back my knife. It won't help you any
more,' the hobgoblin called to him. 'Remember
the old willow lady.'

'That's it!' cried Andrew, and he returned the
knife to the hobgoblin, thanking him nicely for
the use of it. Then, in the middle of the night he
secretly crept into the princess's room and put
a Love-liesbleeding flower into her left slipper.
Early the next morning he stood once more
before the king.

The people rushed to their doors already laughing at the thought of what lady was in store. 'She'll be a fine one that bride of Scarecrow's,' they sneered, eager to make fun of Andrew. However, when a magnificent royal carriage drove on to the village green with Andrew and his lovely princess inside, all those who had mocked Andrew begged him to forgive them. Of course, Andrew did forgive them, for in the end they punished themselves. All the young girls turned green with envy and all the young men's noses turned as red as peonies with their bad tempers. Believe it or not they stayed that way, and that is how you can recognize the village where Andrew was born.

'Do you have them?' asked the king.

'I'm afraid I don't,' answered Andrew and pretended to hang his head in despair.

'I am very sorry for that,' the king said solemnly. 'I am afraid you will have to marry my executioner. What a pity! I was just beginning to like you.'

Just then, the princess ran into the hall, threw open her arms and flung them around Andrew's neck. 'Andrew, my dear Andrew, I love you so much!' she cried and gave the young man kiss after kiss. Their sumptuous wedding lasted 77 days and when they had all danced their fill, Andrew asked his royal bride to go with him in the royal carriage to visit his village. When the royal procession was nearing Andrew's home, the tap of clogs was heard on the village green and the little hobgoblin called into every window,

'Good people all, come quickly outside.

Here comes the Knight Scarecrow and his indent bride.'

Old Lady, Close the Door!

'All fame goes away in the end,' sighed a prince, who wore a little crown of pale mauve flowers. 'In days of old, Arabian beauties used to make up their eyelids, their nails and the tips of their fingers with the splendid yellow colour from my stigmas. Why, even legendary Greek heroes dipped their ceremonial robes in it. Yes, I used to be famous, but that isn't what I wanted to tell you about today. Rather, I'll tell you an Arabian fairy story.'

I know a wonderful country of white mosques and slender minarets. The sun shines there from a boundless sky like a precious, everlasting flower, and during the mild nights, the stars seem to be within arms' reach. When the time comes for prayer, the voice of the prayer caller is carried far, far, right into peoples' hearts. Somewhere in that enchanted country, in the foothills of the mountains, nestles a dazzling white village. In the village is a little cottage and in that cottage an old married couple used to live. They were, indeed, fond of each other, but it was a strange sort of love. As pig-headed as the old man was, so was his wife stubborn, and so their life passed in constant squabbling and argument.

'Old lady, close the door behind us,' the old man would order his wife.

'Me? Why should I? Shut it yourself. You are the one who left it open!' the old lady replied.

'Good Lord!' said the old man irritably. 'How could I leave it open when I didn't open it?'

'That's just like you. You don't even know

how to open the door. All my life I have to be your servant,' the old woman cried.

'What an ass I am!' said the old man furiously. 'I work my fingers to the bone all my life for you, and you can't even open the door for me? That's a fine kettle of fish! You close it!'

'I opened the door, you go and close it!' the old woman shouted.

'There! Now you admit that you opened it,' the old man rejoiced, 'and I didn't, I didn't, I didn't.' They were at it hammer and tongs again. The old man threw his slipper at his wife and the old lady poured a pot of honey over his head. When they were tired of quarrelling, they made peace. That's how it was day after day, from morning till night.

One day the old lady said, 'Listen to me, my man. All our lives we have been squabbling. We are just figures of fun for our neighbours. Come and let's make it up for all time. We'll put on our wedding clothes and make ourselves a feast like when we were young.'

The old man agreed. They put a chicken in the oven to roast. The old lady then painted her eyelids and finger tips with saffron, put on her old wedding dress, put a necklace of saffron flowers around her neck and helped the old man into his clothes. When they were ready, they brought the roast to the table and sat down to enjoy their feast. They smiled at each other.

Before they started eating, the old man said, 'Listen to me, dear wife, it is getting dark and you have left the door open again. What if thieves attacked us in the middle of our meal? Go and close it.' It was as if a wasp had stung the old woman. 'Why should I go and close it? Shut it yourself, you lazy old sluggard!'

'Who's an old sluggard, you ugly old crone?' the old man shouted, furiously banging his fist on the table.

'Please give something to a poor hungry man! Allah will repay you,' he called into the room, but no answer came. The beggar plucked up his courage and went in. Here he saw two figures seated at the table, silent and motionless.

'Goodness me, they must be stuffed,' the beggar thought, and he pinched the old woman's nose till tears came to her eyes. She made not a sound. The beggar pulled the old man's ear till it was red and swollen but he, too, made not a sound. The hungry beggar no longer hesitated. He sat down at the table and set to. How he enjoyed himself. The two old people swallowed, but made no noise at all. Very soon only the bones of the chicken remained. The beggar wiped his greasy mouth, hung the bones on a string and for a joke hung them around the old man's neck. The old man didn't even blink. The beggar just laughed and went on his way.

'You'd better get that door shut right away!'

'When you shut it, it will be shut,' the old woman squawked, flying into a rage. 'All my life I've never been anything more than a drudge to you.'

The old man nearly burst with anger, but he pulled himself together and said, 'We won't get anywhere like that. Do you know what? From now on we'll both sit here in silence, we won't utter a single word. The first to say anything, or even to fidget, must go and close the door. Do you agree?'

The old lady agreed. So there they sat, neither of them making a sound. Only their mouths watered at the sight of the feast both of them had been so looking forward to. A long time passed but neither of them moved. Just then a beggar went by. He noticed the door was open and through it came the lovely smell of roast meat.

Before long, a thief looked in through the open door. He saw the two motionless figures seated at the table.

'Perhaps they are made of wood,' thought the thief. He tickled the old lady under her chin. The old lady said not a word. This suited the thief. He pulled the old man's hair. The old man made not a sound. He filled his sack with whatever he could find, took every last penny the old couple had, and vanished. The old man and old woman cried with misery, but neither one made a move. Just then, a stray dog ran into the room. He was wild and hungry. He smelled the bones and went for the old man's throat.

'May Allah forgive me, that beast will eat my husband!' thought the old lady. She picked up a pan and brought it down on the dog's head. 'Be off with you, you good-for-nothing!' she screamed, as the dog ran out the door. The old man jumped for joy.

'I've won, old lady! Go and close the door!'

So the old lady went to close the door and then she and the old man once more began to argue with relish. They were still arguing when they went to bed, and their insides growled loudly from hunger, too. So now you see what stubborness can lead to.

The Sakura Flower

A white flower was nodding in the breeze on the branch of an ornamental tree. Just then, a wind blew and the flower floated down to the throne of the Rose Queen. Just as it touched the crystal floor, it turned into a delicate little girl. She greeted the Rose Queen solemnly, waving her fan of white cherry flowers, and said, 'I, the daughter of Sakura, the Japanese Cherry, humbly ask permission to tell a story from the Land of the Rising Sun.'

Far, far away there is a country by the shores of which lies the cradle of the sun, hidden deep in the ocean. A poor mountain peasant used to live in this country. His name was Tadakichi. Every day, he wandered over the hills and dales gathering dry wood which he carried down into the valley. This daily trail barely gave him enough to live on.

When he lay down at night, he thought bitterly, 'What is the use of such a life when a man is rarely at home. The fire is always out, the house untidy, no one is here to smile at me or to cry over me. If I had a kind, loving wife, life would be much better.'

One day, his wish was fulfilled. Unexpectedly, an attractive woman came to his door. She smiled at him and said, 'I know that your name is Tadakichi. You are alone in the world and that is not good for a man. I am also alone. Please let me stay with you. I will work hard and will cost you nothing. I don't need any food all day long and I promise that I will take good care of you.'

Tadakichi could not believe his eyes and ears. He had never dreamed of such a good-looking helpmate and companion. He wasted no time in reaching a decision. 'If you are speaking the truth, I shall be glad to keep you here. Loneliness is as bad as want. Perhaps we shall get on well together.'

Tadakichi was right. It was obvious from the very beginning that the woman was a hard worker. She rushed about like a whirlwind, nothing was too much for her and day after day she prepared the tastiest food for Tadakichi. She herself did not even lick her finger. Tadakichi could not understand it.

'Upon my soul, perhaps that woman really does live off the wind and water,' he wondered, 'and all the time she is so full of energy. I can't understand it.'

After a while, however, he began to get suspicious and looking into the chest where he kept a store of rice for the winter, he discovered it was almost empty.

'Look what a thief she is,' he complained.

'She behaves like an innocent and behind my back, she is stuffing herself like a glutton. I'll have to keep a look out and catch her in the act.'

The next day, when the woman was preparing his breakfast in the morning, he told her that he had to go on a long journey. 'I won't be back before evening,' he said and set out, apparently, for the mountains. After a while, though, he turned off the road and crept back unobserved. He hid himself and waited to see what would happen. He had not long to wait. As soon as the woman was sure that he was gone, she opened the chest, took out the rest of the rice and started cooking. Soup was merrily bubbling in the pot, the rice was steaming, the fire crackled and the woman was singing a strange song. It

sounded like a witch's spell. Her song gave Tadakichi the shivers.

When the rice was cooked, the woman made little balls of it, tipped the soup into a dish and them she threw back her hair from the top of her head. Tadakichi's blood froze in his veins, for the woman had a huge pair of jaws on her head and into those jaws she threw the rice balls, one after another, and then poured in the hot soup. Finally she even ate what Tadakichi had left on his plate that morning. Then she combed her hair nicely and rested after her feast. At last Tadakichi understood how things were. Why, it was no other than the evil witch Jamamba! The poor fellow was so terrified, he jumped head first into an empty barrel used for rain water and did not dare to show even the tip of his nose. There he stayed until evening.

When he did not return home even after dark, the witch became suspicious. It occurred to her that there was something odd about his journey to the mountains. She searched the cottage inside and out, but found nothing. Calling in a small, sweet voice she said, 'Tadakichi, my dear husband, have you come back yet?' 'Not yet,' the confused Tadakichi cried from the barrel. The witch laughed.

'Then I am not going to wait for you. I don't like it here with you, but I'll take this old barrel as a souvenir,' and before Tadakichi realized what she was doing, Jamamba hauled the barrel on to her back and hurried up into the mountains. On the way, she smashed rocks, pulled up trees and shouted noisily, 'All you witches, my dear sisters, get a fire ready. I am bringing you a nice roast in this barrel such as you have never

before tasted. How we are going to enjoy it!'

Tadakichi did not know what to do. 'My dear and beautiful trees, please help me,' he called. 'I have broken off your dead branches, I have covered your roots with dried leaves to protect them, now have pity on me,' and the trees heard his call. They bent their branches and pulled the poor man out of the barrel. The witch did not notice anything and rushed on up into the mountains. Tadakichi waited for nothing. He raced towards home like a hare. When the witch reached her mountain cave and found that Tadakichi had escaped, she screamed with temper and trampled the barrel into splinters. Then she hurled herself down into the valley after the poor man who was still running. In a moment she was at his heels. Her claws were reaching for him and all her teeth gnashed in the

/ 191 /

jaws on top of her head. Tadakichi had just reached the pond and here a bright idea came to him. He jumped from the path into the rushes and reeds, crouched down and held his breath. Jamamba roared in anger. She knew as well as Tadakichi that if she were to step among these plants, her witch's legs would at once fall off. So she considered what to do. Three times she turned on her heel and so doing, changed back into a lovely girl.

'Come on out my husband, we'll dance together,' she said enticingly, but he only laughed and waited patiently for the witch to go away and leave him alone.

From that time, in that far away land, when the time of the Boys' Festival comes, they hang bunches of reeds on the eaves and put reeds into their baths in memory of Tadakichi's escape from the witch. It helps to protect them from the evil Jamamba and all unclean forces.

The Spectre Uwa-Uwa

The proud princess Orchid came before the Rose Queen in tears. 'I am feeling homesick,' she cried. 'We orchids are from the hot south. Members of my family bloom in steamy jungles all over the world. I was born on a beautiful island dotted with crystal-clear lakes and pure springs where Rajah Rimba, king of the forest and leader of the elephants, goes to drink. I will tell you a story from the island.'

Very close to the dense jungle, there lived a poor widower with his small son Yantho. When his wife was dying, she said to him, 'Never neglect our little son. I am entrusting him to your loving care. Pray for him and guard him against the evil demons of the jungle. Even though you might be dying of hunger, you must share your last grain of rice with him. Do not forget my words.'

The man did not take her words to heart. He was a bad and lazy man. He got out of work when he could and liked best of all to wander around and get drunk on rice wine. It is not surprising that want was soon on their doorstep. Here and there he managed to beg a handful of rice from sympathetic people, but he nearly always ate it all himself, only rarely sharing with

his poor little son. Little Yantho often cried with hunger.

When things were at their worst, the little boy ran to the edge of the jungle and bowing deeply, spoke these words. 'Para wanara, wise family of monkeys, I, the wretched Yantho, son of man, am calling to you. Please throw down a nut from your trees.'

When they heard his call, the monkeys always took pity and answered Yantho's request. Monkeys are not reliable, however, and often their games and their chasing took them to another part of the jungle. Then little Yantho, terrified, would peep into the tangle of lianas, calling, 'Oh noble Harimau, free-running tiger and lord of the shadows! The wretched Yantho, hungry son of man, begs you for a small share in your spoils.'

The tiger felt sorry for the starving little boy and shared his prey with Yantho. The ways of the tiger are also inconstant and take the striped hunter far into the depths of the jungle. So it happened that at times Yantho got no answer to his call. When he came home empty handed, his father treated him cruelly.

'You are good for nothing, you lazy creature,' the man cursed and hit the boy so hard that he fell down. 'You are unable to provide even a mouthful of proper food for your father.'

One day, the father succeeded in begging a handful of rice from somewhere. 'Why should I always share my last grain with that nitwit?' he thought angrily. 'I'll take him deep into the jungle and leave him there at the mercy of the wild animals.'

The next day, Yantho's father woke him early. No sooner said that done. He told the boy that they were going into the jungle to gather dry wood for sale and Yantho trustingly went with him. When they came to the edge of the jungle they were stopped by a thick tangle of lianas, but the boy bowed deeply and spoke these words, 'Para wanara, family of monkeys, this is me, Yantho, the little son of man, I am going with my father to collect a bundle of firewood. Please open for us a way into the jungle.' Lo and behold! Like a miracle, the lianas parted.

Soon after, however, the wanderers were stopped by a dense thicket of thorn bushes. The boy then called, 'Oh noble tiger Harimau, lord of the shadows! I, little Yantho, son of man, am asking you to open up the way for us.'

At that moment, the thorny bushes parted and the tiger path took them deep into the dark jungle. In the middle of a little clearing the father stopped at last, made a fire and poured the handful of rice into a pan of water.

'Before we start work, let us take a rest and have a meal,' he said to his son, but when the rice was cooked, he ate it all himself, leaving just one grain at the bottom of the pan.

'Wait here for me,' he ordered the boy. 'I am going to look around to find where there are a lot of dry branches and roots. When I come back, we'll share that last grain of rice, as your mother wished.'

With that, he disappeared into the jungle. Yantho crouched beside the fire, hungry and frightened, but he did not dare taste the grain of rice for fear of angering his father. While he waited for his father, he fed the fire with dry branches, and spread the ash. With his dirty hands he wiped away his tears, and soon his face was dirty also. Yantho waited a long time, but his father did not come. Darkness fell. The evil eyes of invisible predators shone in the darkness behind him, and the frightened child could hear the hissing of poisonous snakes and the creeping tread of hunting beasts. It seemed to

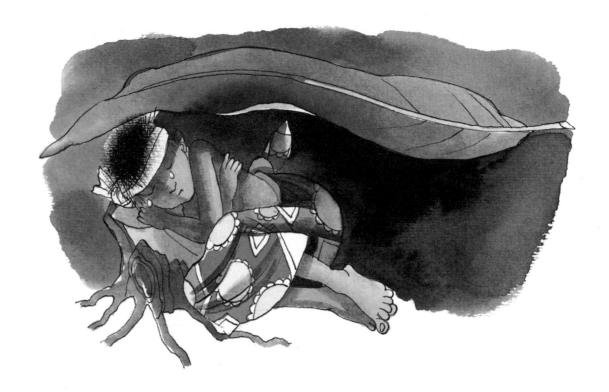

Yantho that the demons of the jungle were hiding in the dark shadows.

'Uwa-uwa,' the boy cried. 'Come back, father, uwa-uwa!' Yantho's father was absolutely nowhere to be seen, however, and in the end, Yantho plucked up his courage and went to look for him in the mysterious darkness of the jungle. Meanwhile, the treacherous man was hurrying homeward but he, too, was soon overtaken by darkness. In his great haste, he fell into the spiky thorn bushes, which had once again closed across the path.

'Open up for me your tiger path, oh noble hunter Harimau,' he called. 'I have left a tasty prey for you in the jungle.'

From the darkness the tiger roared his reply, 'Go back for your son, you treacherous man! A free hunter is not interested in human flesh.'

Yantho's father did not give up so easily. 'Para wanara, family of monkeys, guide me out of the dark jungle. I, the father of the little boy Yantho, am calling to you.'

A blinding light then pierced the darkness and the monkey king appeared to the terrified man. He was sitting on a pile of diamonds and in his hands held a coconut. 'Go where my coconut leads you,' said the monkey king and he hurled the nut at the man's feet. The coconut took off on its own, rolling through the bushes and thickets, forging a way for the treacherous father. It did not lead out of the jungle, but back to the place he was running away from. Before long, the man saw the dying fire. The last grain of rice glittered at the bottom of the pan beside it. Greedily, the man reached out his hand for it, but just then a strange creature emerged from the gloom of the jungle. Eyes like precious jewels shone from its black face and from its mouth came a ghostly wail.

'Uwa-uwa,' the little spectre cried. 'Uwa-

uwa,' it wailed. The grain of rice stuck in the man's throat.

'A demon!' he yelled and tried to run away. Just then, orchid flowers glowed in the trees as though a thousand stars had come out in the sky. In the most beautiful of the flowers the face of Yantho's mother appeared.

'You did not keep your word,' the apparition said. 'You have not cared for our little son, not shared your food with him. You have been a cruel and heartless father and for that, you will fall victim to the jungle. From now on you will become a demon in animal skin. You will wander in misery through the jungle until a kindly person shares his last grain of rice with you.'

A strange sensation overcame the man as he realized that his body was becoming covered

with animal fur. Sharp claws grew from his hands and feet and a green light gleamed in his eyes.

'Uwa-uwa,' the unhappy man wailed and he ran off into the jungle.

'Uwa-uwa,' cried the little spectre he had left behind. Of course, it was not a spectre but poor little Yantho.

'Pick my orchid flower,' said the voice of his mother. 'It will guide you safely home.' Yantho obeyed and the radiant flower guided him along the dark jungle paths, right to the threshold of the palm-leaf hut. The lovely flower is as fresh and vibrant now as it always was, and whenever Yantho is troubled, his mother's face appears in it. She sings to him and soothes him with her sweet perfume.

Since then Yantho's father has wandered through the jungle and on dark nights a sorrowful wailing can be heard from the undergrowth. 'Uwa-uwa, Uwa-uwa,' it cries as the enchanted beast tries in vain to find the way home, and Yantho goes to the edge of the jungle with a single grain of rice to share with his unhappy father. Perhaps one day they will meet and the spell will be broken.

Simpleton

Vain Narcissus sat sighing at his reflection in a crystal mirror.

'What sort of story will you tell us?' the Rose Queen asked him.

'I'll tell you the story of how one day I saw my own lovely face in the well and how I fell in love with it.'

'Oh no!' the flowers cried all together. 'Everyone knows that story. We have heard it at least a hundred times. Let Princess Cornflower tell us her story instead.' Narcissus turned away offended and blue-eyed Cornflower began her story.

There was once a very poor man living in a little cottage. Simpleton was his name. His parents would often sigh, 'Our dear son Simpleton, when brains were being given out, you came after our tomcat. Before your turn, he licked the heavenly pot clean of every last crumb of wisdom. He has more sense in his tail then you have in your knobbly head. When we are gone, take good care of yourself and before you make any decisions, you'd better tap your head three times. Perhaps it will light up.'

Well, Simpleton was an obedient son and when one sad day he found himself alone in the world, he made up his mind to stick by their advice. Once, in summer, he went out into the fields to see how his grain was ripening. Suddenly, a little dwarf appeared in front of him. His clothes were all meadow flowers and

on his head was a bluebell cap. He was scowling awfully.

'What's up with you, little chap?' kind-hearted Simpleton asked him.

'I've got the weight of the world on my shoulders,' he answered. 'My bride-to-be, a flower fairy, wants me to bring her the blue of the sky, for her skirt. How am I to do that when I am so small? If you could help me, I would pay you well.'

Simpleton racked his brains but he couldn't think of anything. Then he tapped his head three times, as his parents advised him, and at once his head lit up.

'I've got it!' he cried and from among the wheat spikes, he plucked a lovely flowering cornflower. 'This is what you want. A little piece of the blue of the sky.'

The dwarf was overjoyed. 'Why ever didn't it occur to me? It will make a fine skirt for a bride. Take this for your good advice,' he said and placed a handful of little seeds into Simpleton's palm. 'When you plough your field in the autumn, plant it with these seeds. You will see that they will bring you good luck,' he said and disappeared without trace.

Simpleton did as the dwarf said. When it was time for autumn sowing, he scattered the seeds over the ground and every day he looked to see if they had begun to grow. Spring came and the green shoots appeared. Then came summer and the ears ripened. Simpleton was eager for the harvest. He was the first in the village to take up his scythe and go off to the field. He picked the first ear to test it and rubbed it in his palms to see if the grain was ripe. He picked a second and a third. To Simpleton's surprise, instead of wheat grains, each ear contained grains of pure gold! Simpleton sat down on the side of the field and burst into tears.

'That dratted dwarf! How could he cheat me like this?' he moaned. 'What shall I do now? Who will grind me fine white flour from grains of gold? What shall I bake cakes from in the winter? Oh poor me, this is such bad luck!'

Just then the wily miller passed by. He realized at once what was going on, and decided to take advantage of it.

'Listen Simpleton,' he said. 'That is bad luck. I am not surprised you are crying over such a crop. Let me tell you something. Because I am a kind soul, I'll help you. I'll buy all that gold grain off you for a sack of flour.'

Simpleton jumped with joy and he shook hands with the miller on it. 'There's nothing better than a good bargain,' he thought delightedly. He loaded the sack on his back and started out for home. On the way he met an old bird-catcher who carried on a cart cages full of the loveliest song birds you could imagine. Simpleton liked one of them in particular.

'What do you want for that most beautiful one?' he inquired. 'A sack of flour,' answered the bird-catcher. Simpleton didn't think twice.

'There's nothing better than a good bargain,' he said with pleasure. He gave the bird-catcher the sack of flour and started on his way home with the bird. Remembering his promise to his mother and father he tapped his head three times and his head lit up.

'Wait a minute, fellow-me-lad! What will we eat, my lovely bird and I, when we haven't even a handful of flour? As sure as Simpleton is my name, I'll find a solution. I'll sell the empty cage back to the bird-catcher. Wait here for me, you lovely song bird,' Simpleton said and he took the bird out of the cage, sat him on a dogrose bush and ran after the bird-catcher.

'Hey, my good man,' he called, all out of breath. 'What will you give me if I sell your cage back to you?'

'What should I give you?' the bird-catcher grinned. 'Didn't you say yourself that the cage is mine? Give it back to me quickly or I'll have you thrown into jail.'

Simpleton was so startled that he did as he was told and gave the empty cage back to the bird-catcher. Sadly he walked home. On the way, he looked for his bird but it was nowhere to be seen. So the unhappy Simpleton went back to his cottage empty handed. He sat on the doorstep and lamented, 'Oh, that nasty dwarf! I gave him the blue of the sky and the ungrateful creature ruined me completely. That's how the world goes.'

Luckily for Simpleton, he found three grains of pure gold that had fallen into his boot. 'Perhaps some stupid person will give me something for them,' he thought and took them to the market in the town. With them he brought a sack of grain, a hen, a goose and a lump of butter.

'It's a good thing I know how to drive a hard bargain,' thought Simpleton smugly and some-how he managed to live through the winter contentedly. He truly was a Simpleton!

The Brave Flower Girl

A handsome young man with rosy cheeks bowed deeply to the Rose Queen. 'I am Carnation, a flower linked with legend and fame. Ladies have given me to soldiers on their way to battle. Handsome young men and beautiful young women have exchanged my flowers as a sweet sign of love. I have been the symbol of freedom, of bravery and of beauty. Now, instead of all that, I want to tell you a story about some people who cared for me, above all other flowers.'

Many, many years ago in a far off little town, there lived a young flower girl called Katie and her small brother. The little flower girl and her brother were all alone in the world. Life was not easy for Katie, but she did her best to care for her brother and her flower garden. When her work at home was done, she went to the market with a song on her lips to sell her lovely carnations. They smelled so sweet that people almost became dizzy with the fragrance.

One day, when Katie was getting her flower basket ready, she said to her little brother, 'Now be a good boy and don't wander off anywhere.

I don't want to have to search for you this evening somewhere in the meadows.'

The boy promised he would not wander off, but hardly had she left when he felt himself drawn to the forest. On the way he made himself a whistle from a willow wand and playing a merry tune, he wandered off wherever his feet took him. Before long he found himself deep in the dark forest. Soon he came to the bank of a silent pool carpeted with water lilies. It was so quiet all round that he felt a tingle of fear in his spine. To chase the fear away, he began to play even more cheerful tunes on his whistle. The water lily flowers opened and out of each one peeped an astonished nymph.

'Who is that playing so beautifully?' they asked each other and when they noticed the lonely boy, they floated on lily leaves to the bank and began to dance.

'More, more!' they cried and the boy played and played until it began to get dark.'

'More, more!' the nymphs demanded.

'I have to go home. My sister will be worried about me, and I am afraid of the dark.'

The nymphs tried in vain to persuade him, and when he would not be persuaded, they were angry. 'You are afraid of the dark, you foolish boy? So be it. From this moment on may you see nothing else but darkness,' cried the eldest nymph and she brushed her long hair across his eyes. At once the boy was surrounded by inky blackness. He looked up to the sky to see the stars, but there was only endless darkness. The boy began to cry.

'I am blind!' he wailed and tried to run home to tell his dear sister, but he did not know which way to turn. He wandered here and there through the deep forest, fell into ditches and scratched his hands on thorns. Suddenly, the wind brought with it the smell of carnations. He turned towards the scent and after a long time, he reached home.

'Oh, you poor boy. What has happened to you?' she cried. 'How shall we live now? I won't be able to let you out of my sight!'

Katie was right. A time of great trouble had come upon her. Whenever she wanted to go to the market, she had to carry her little brother on her back so that he did not have to remain at home alone and helpless. Soon, however, the boy learned to walk blindly after the scent of her flowers and so Katie never left home without a little bunch of carnations. She took the boy on long walks into the fields and meadows to try and cheer him up, but nothing seemed to work and he grew sadder and sadder.

'I shall never see the sun again. I shall never see your lovely flowers,' he wailed. Katie's heart was heavy. One day she decided to go with the boy to the water lily pool to ask the nymphs for mercy.

'Take a holy candle with you. That will protect you against everything evil,' a wise neighbour advised her.

Katie did as her neighbour advised. She picked a fresh bunch of carnations and set out for the dark forest with her blind brother. When, after a long search, she found the water lily pool, she lit the candle and asked her brother to start playing on his whistle. As soon

Deep at the bottom of the pool is a golden snake. He is guarding two shells and in each of them is a rainbow pearl. If you could manage to bring the pearls to the top and place them on your brother's eyes, he would see again. Let the boy put the snake to sleep with a soft lullaby. Then you will be able to enter the pool, but beware of waking the snake, for if you do, he will kill you!'

Kate did as she knew she must. She told the boy to play a soft lullaby on his willow whistle and fearlessly she stepped into the pool, still holding the lit candle. By some magic, the flame did not go out in the water, and its light guided the brave girl though the gloom to the bottom of the pool. To Katie's astonishment, she found that she could breathe in this pool, just as easily as she was able to in the open air.

The body of the golden snake glistened in the black mud at the bottom of the pool. It was sleeping soundly and near its head lay two shells, each containing a rainbow pearl, just as the nymph had said. Katie moved silently and stretched out her hand to the shells. Just then the boy on the bank stopped playing. The snake woke suddenly from its sleep and like lightning, wound itself around the girl's neck. She could feel her life draining slowly away. Her strength failing, she cried weakly, 'Play, little brother, play. Don't leave your faithful sister in the power of the evil snake.'

The boy heard her and once more began to play his soft lullaby. The golden snake closed its eyes, released its grip and fell back to the bottom of the pool. The girl quickly grabbed the rainbow pearls and hurried back to the bank. There she placed the pearls on the boy's eyes.

'Katie, I can see again!' the happy boy cried and threw his arms around his sister. The oldest nymph then stood before them.

as he played the first notes, the water lily flowers opened and the nymphs hurried to the bank on water lily leaves. At once they started to dance. They danced nearer and nearer until the oldest of them was within arm's reach of Katie. Katie reached out and caught hold of the nymph by her long dark hair.

'You wicked enchantress,' Katie cried. 'I won't let you go until you return my brother's sight.'

The nymph was frightened. 'Do please forgive me. I am sorry now for what I have done, but I don't know how to return your brother's sight. If you are brave, I will tell you what to do.

'Please sell me your red carnation,' she said. I should like to weave in into my hair. I'll pay you well for it.'

Katie handed her the carnation, and in return the nymph gave her a generous handful of fish scales. 'Guard them well,' said the nymph. 'They will bring you luck.'

The girl laughed. 'What should we do with ordinary fish scales,' she thought and when she returned home with her brother, she wanted to throw them away, but wonder of wonders! The scales had turned to gold. Katie had no desire for gold, however, and one day she and her brother paid another visit to the water lily pool.

'Please take your gift back, dear nymph,' she called and poured the scales into the pool. 'Our love and the lovely flowers from our garden are enough for us two to be happy.'

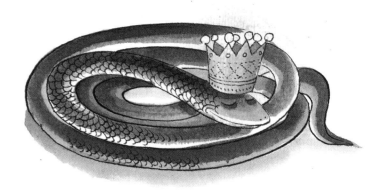

In the water, the golden scales turned into little gold fish which disappeared under the surface. The water lily flowers opened and the lovely nymphs waved goodbye to brave Katie and her little brother. No one has ever seen them since.

The Flowers Go Home

The last story ended and the Rose Queen lifted her head in alarm. 'Did you hear that? What was it?' she whispered.

Every one listened intently. 'Pipes! The Pipes of Pan are calling to us. Spring is returning to the world of people!' little Snowdrop cried and hurried to the door. 'Please forgive me. I mustn't be late. My time has come,' she called and waved her slender hand for the last time.

The Rose Queen sighed. 'What a pity, the ball is over. We must now say goodbye to each other.'

The flowers lingered. 'What about our stories? Which one was the best?' they called.

'Let the children decide,' the Queen smiled, 'when you are blooming in the meadows and gardens, they will come to enjoy your beauty. Tell them, then, in your silent language, your strange stories. It will give them pleasure. I wish you all a pleasant journey back to the world of people.'

Then the flowers departed gracefully, one after the other.